BOOK I OF THE
HUNTERS' GIRL SERIES

THE HUNTERS' GIRL

BARB HENDEE

COPYRIGHT

.   .   .   .   .

Print, eBook and Cover Design by
N.D. Author Services [NDAS]
www.NDAuthorServices.com

.   .   .   .   .

Cover Art by
BetiBup33 Studio Design
www.betibupp33.com

CONTENTS

Chapter One: The Job.............................1

Chapter Two: The Ghost.........................13

Chapter Three: The Nest........................29

Chapter Four: The Girl..........................59

Chapter Five: The Trial Run....................75

Chapter Six: The Empath........................91

Chapter Seven: The Hotel.......................101

Chapter Eight: The Angry Man..................111

Chapter Nine: The Possession..................123

Chapter Ten: Victoria..........................135

Chapter Eleven: The Ring.......................167

Chapter Twelve: Home...........................173

About the Author...............................181

CHAPTER ONE:

THE JOB

C ooper Reyes wasn't lazy. He'd managed to earn his own money since the age of sixteen and was no stranger to hard work. But somehow, he just wasn't wired to work a nine-to-five job. For him, it wasn't so much the hours as it was being tied to certain place without being able to leave. He'd tried everything from a lumber mill to working at a Jiffy Lube changing the oil in cars (thinking this might provide more variety), but nothing felt right. Each moment he spent stuck in any *one* place made the skin at the back of his neck start to itch until all he could think about was leaving.

By odd luck, in his early twenties, this led him to a job as a bounty hunter, and a few years later, by even odder luck, that led to him starting his own business with a partner... hunting things that nobody else wanted to hunt. Sure, the money was spotty, and he never knew when the next job might turn up, but he always paid his bills, and the skin at the back of his neck never itched anymore.

In early March, on a Tuesday morning, between jobs, he was out behind the log cabin in Quinault, Washington, where he lived, splitting wood for the stove, when he heard the back door open and close again. Half turning, he lowered his axe to see his business partner, Lee Nevada, walking toward him through the trees.

"Just got a call," Lee said, still holding a phone in his hand.

"Sound legit?"

"Maybe. But we'll need to drive to Idaho."

Though both men were tall, over six feet, and in their late twenties, they were a sharp contrast otherwise. Cooper's father was from a Salish tribe of Washington State, and his mother was a natural blonde. He'd inherited his father's dark hair and his mother's blue eyes. While slender, he was a good deal stronger than he looked. He'd grown up in the Pacific Northwest and had never known a life without rain, moss, and evergreen trees.

Lee, on the other hand, looked like a cross between a soldier and an all-American football player. His jaw was solid, and he carried his strength in his arms and chest. After a six-year stint in the army, he still wore his sandy-colored hair short. He'd grown up in Georgia, the sixth of seven children, and spoke with a slight Southern lilt. But he'd never liked heat or steamy humidity, and on his first visit to northwest Washington, he'd quickly decided he was never going back.

"So, what are we talking?" Cooper asked.

"Ghost."

Cooper nodded. Ghosts accounted for most of their paying jobs. In the past year and a half, the two of them had hunted everything from vampires to werewolves to shifters to the occasional animated corpse. But those jobs were fewer and farther between. Ghosts paid for the property taxes, groceries, beer, and put gas in the tank.

Setting down the axe, he followed Lee back into the cabin. Although they called it a cabin, as it was made from logs, in truth, it was more of an old two-story house, with a kitchen, living room, bathroom, and large bedroom downstairs, and three bedrooms and a bathroom upstairs. Cooper had inherited it from his grandmother.

Neither he nor Lee cared much about décor (or housekeeping), so the place tended to be somewhat of a mess, with beer cans lining the kitchen counter and dishes piled in the sink. They played poker once a week to see who would get stuck cleaning the bathrooms. The wiring needed repair, and they couldn't use the microwave and the toaster at the same time. Besides a few space heaters, the main heat source was a wood stove. But the place was home, and it suited them both fine. It had everything they needed, including cell phone service and high-speed internet.

Lee walked to the kitchen table and picked up a canvas backpack, which already appeared to be stuffed with necessary supplies and equipment. Then he lifted a sawed-off shotgun from its place on the wall.

"Where in Idaho?" Cooper asked.

"Few miles outside of Boise."

Cooper nodded.

.   .   .   .   .

Less than an hour later, as they were driving into Aberdeen, Cooper slowed for traffic.

On jobs, they always drove his 2003 Jeep Cherokee. Though it was seventeen years old, with over 160,000 miles, it was more dependable than Lee's old Ford pickup, which tended to break down at inopportune times.

"So, what do we know?" Cooper asked.

"This one could get bad. Got a couple of dead pets already," Lee answered, leaning back on the passenger side. "Client's name is Mary Faulkner. She and her wife—"

"Wife?"

"Yup."

Cooper nodded. He didn't judge. "Go on."

"She and her wife bought an older house to remodel. Everything was fine until last week when they were working in the basement and broke through a locked door into a storage room, as they didn't have a key. They must have woke something up 'cause the trouble started that night."

When Lee spoke, he always elongated the first syllable in words like "everything," but he also dropped the 'y.'

"More than just screams in the night, I'm guessing?" Cooper asked.

"Yeah. Dishes and pans flying in the kitchen. TV going on and off. They found their parakeet dead first, frozen solid to the bottom of its cage. Yesterday, they found their dog on the kitchen floor... same, frozen solid."

Cooper winced. It always bothered him when pets paid such a price. "Any actual sightings?"

"Not yet, but the women moved out after finding the dog," Lee said. "They're staying in town. I've got both addresses."

"How'd they find us?" Cooper asked.

"The website."

"Good."

When they'd first launched the business, Cooper created a website advertising their services. He chose the name Permanent Solutions Unnatural, thinking there was a nice ring to it. He always liked to know how and where people learned of their... expertise. And he preferred clients who went through the website—as this kept things more professional. There was a contact email address, but people nearly always called instead of writing. Most of their clients were desperate and shaken, and they liked to hear another voice when asking for help. This was understandable.

"How soon is Ms. Faulkner expecting us?" he asked.

"Tomorrow. I knew we had a ten-hour drive ahead, and we'd need some sleep tonight."

"Good," Cooper said again.

Clients paid for travel expenses, but only after the initial interview and the client had officially engaged the services of Permanent Solutions Unnatural. Still, in the year and a half that Cooper and Lee had been running the business, after the initial interview, no one had ever decided not to hire them.

· · · · · ·

About ten-thirty that night, they pulled into Boise and found a room with two beds in a Quality Inn. Cooper was thinking about ordering a large pizza and having it delivered. Now that they'd secured accommodations for the night, he didn't feel like getting back in the Jeep —or even leaving the room.

But within a few minutes of stepping through the door, Lee set down his gear and paced restlessly.

"I think I'll go out for a while," he said. "Find a bar."

Cooper was well aware this was a euphemism for hooking up with a woman, but he was used to Lee's tendencies when they traveled. Lee liked women, and they liked him. He wasn't the settling down type, and he never pretended otherwise. He never lied about himself, and he made it clear he was only interested in a night or two at most, and yet he still always managed to get laid.

Cooper shook his head in wonder at the thought. He'd had a few girlfriends—though no one right now. But he couldn't recall a single woman in his life who'd made it past the second date before asking, "So, where do you see this relationship going?"

"Okay," he said, sitting on a bed and pulling a silver laptop computer from his bag. "Just leave me the address of the house with the haunting. I'll do some digging online and see what I can find for a history. Oh, and make sure you bring your key so you can get back in. I'm going to order some food, but once I'm done with dinner and a little research, I want to get some sleep."

Lee cocked his head. "I already texted you the address, and I'll thank you to remember that I've forgotten my hotel key only once."

"Yeah, and you were banging on the door at three-thirty in the morning, drunk and yelling to get back in. The manager almost threw us out."

"Will I ever live that down?"

"Nope." Cooper fired up his computer and connected to the Wi-Fi.

Lee flashed a grin. "Well, it would have been worth getting thrown out. You should have seen the girl I was with that night."

"You've told me all about her, more than once."

"I'll see what I can find tonight."

Cooper didn't look up from the screen. "Just be back by mid-morning."

"I always am."

Lee sauntered out the door as Cooper glanced at his phone and then began typing in the address of the house they'd be exploring tomorrow.

.   .   .   .   .

It was light when Lee woke up the next morning, and for a few seconds, he couldn't remember where he was. Then he smelled strawberry shampoo and looked down to see a dark-haired woman sleeping with her head on his chest. He recalled liking the scent of her hair the night before.

They were in her apartment, in her bed. Through the window, he could see it was full daylight outside.

"Jennifer," he said softly, not wanting to disturb her, but worrying about the time. Though they'd just met last night, he always made it a point to memorize a woman's name and believed this to be common manners. "I need to go pick up my partner. We've got a meeting this morning."

She murmured something about making him coffee but then rolled off his chest instead, going back to sleep. With some relief, he slid out of the bed. Goodbyes had never been his strong suit.

Once on his feet, he dressed quickly into jeans, a T-shirt, laced boots, and a canvas jacket. Upon leaving the apartment, he found the Jeep parked on the street. Though he'd never admit it to Cooper, he liked traveling in the Jeep. It was silver with black seats, and Cooper took good care of it. Glancing at his watch, Lee saw it was nearly ten-thirty and pulled out his phone, hitting the first number at the top of his list.

"Where are you?" Cooper answered.

"On my way. Ten minutes. Meet me out front."

They both hung up. Lee hopped into the Jeep, started the engine, and pulled out into morning traffic. Boise had grown up over the years into a fair-sized city, but he wasn't far from the hotel. He'd arranged to meet Mary Faulkner this morning at eleven o'clock, and he knew they'd be on time. He took his job seriously. He took Cooper's trust seriously. His life was better now than it had ever been, and he had no intention of doing anything to jeopardize his home or the friendship.

Whenever he thought back to his childhood, the phrase that most often came to mind was "dirt poor." His mother had been slender and beautiful and big-hearted... with the worst taste in men. She owned a three-bedroom trailer in a park just outside of Savannah, Georgia. Lee's father had been her third husband, but Lee didn't remember him, as the man was gone by the time Lee turned two years old. By the time he was three, his mother was married to husband number four... and like all the men before him, he moved into the trailer as opposed to providing a home. Not long after this, her seventh child (a baby girl) was born. Two adults and seven children living in a three-bedroom trailer had been a lot like too many animals crowded into the same cage.

Lee's youth consisted of often going to school with no breakfast and no packed lunch while suffering looks of either contempt or pity from his teachers. And yet, through all this, his mother couldn't seem to stop trying to help anyone or anything in need. Some of the children in the trailer park were worse off than her own, and she fed them when she could. The same went for stray dogs or cats or anything that crossed her path. Once, she let a homeless man sleep on their makeshift porch for an entire summer.

Some days, Lee wanted to scream at her to take care of her own, but she was gentle and still beautiful, and he loved her.

At eighteen, he joined the army and did two tours in Afghanistan. When he couldn't bring himself to re-enlist, he'd gone home with no idea what to do with his life. Then one night, tragedy struck his family, and as a result, he'd met Cooper. A whole new world opened for him, and everything changed.

Weaving through Boise traffic, he spotted Cooper waiting for him outside the hotel, dressed in near identical clothing: boots, jeans, T-shirt, and a canvas jacket. Packs of gear lay at his feet, and he carried the shotgun in his left hand.

Lee pulled up so Cooper could load their gear and climb into the passenger side.

"Nice night?" Cooper asked.

"No complaints," Lee answered, heading out of the parking lot back toward the street. "You find anything on the house?"

"Not much. It was repossessed about six years ago, and it's been on the market since. Mary Faulkner just bought it last month."

"Six years empty?"

"Yeah. It's miles outside of town, but it didn't come with any real property, and from the photos online, it looked like it needed a lot of work."

Lee smiled. "Mary and her wife must have wanted try their hand. We'll see if we can't clean it out for them."

He liked to view what they did as helpful to other people, even though they charged their clients money. Cooper handled the finances, and he was a whiz. He was the one who'd incorporated their business as something he called an "LLC," though Lee didn't fully understand what that meant. With a ghost hunt, Cooper normally charged twenty-five hundred a day plus expenses. It rarely took them longer than a day to handle a restless spirit, but even if they managed to land only three jobs in a month, that was seventy-five hundred dollars. Cooper divided their money four ways. He had a house account for things like property taxes, electricity, and basic groceries. He had another account for income taxes—which had baffled Lee until Cooper explained a necessity called "quarterly tax payments." The remaining money was divided equally between them.

Lee found the arrangement more than equitable, as it left him with an income and almost no bills, and he was grateful to Cooper for handling all this. Cooper even used a contract with their clients, and he'd had a lawyer help write it. In addition to a legal agreement for payment for services rendered, the contract absolved them from any unavoidable property damage. When hunting the types of *things* that they hunted, broken furniture or bullet holes in the walls were an occupational hazard. Their clients needed to recognize this.

"Where are Mary and her wife staying now?" Cooper asked.

"At their previous home here in Boise. They still haven't sold it." Lee had memorized the address, and he turned down a side street of neat but older homes from the 1980s. All the lawns were carefully mowed. "Just up here."

. . . . .

Ten minutes later, Cooper found himself sitting beside Lee at a kitchen table while he tried to get the measure of their potential clients.

Mary was a tall woman, nearly as tall as him, with short brown hair and a smattering of freckles. She wore a plaid flannel shirt over faded jeans and had a no-nonsense air. Her wife, Amy, was a small, slightly rounded woman with curly red hair. But she appeared somewhat lost and shaken. Her hand trembled when she poured them all cups of coffee.

"Cream or sugar?" she asked.

"No, thank you, ma'am," Lee answered, letting his Southern accent thicken a little. "We both take it black."

Mary was sizing them up. "So, you two actually do what your website says? You can clear out a ghost?" She shook her head. "I've never heard of anything like this in real life, and I don't hold with those reality TV shows about spirit hunters... some yahoos chasing around inside an old house with a video camera."

Cooper was accustomed to this. Upon encountering something unnatural plaguing their life, most people were frightened at first, but they soon turned angry at the prospect of even *having* to hire someone to take care of the problem.

"Mary," Amy said softly. "These men haven't brought any video cameras. And you read the testimonials to me from their website."

Cooper was proud of the testimonials. Four clients had written reviews of their work for him to post on the site. Every word of the reviews was true, and because they were true, they read like the truth. These reviews had gained them a good deal of business.

Mary made a huffing sound. "So, what exactly will you do inside our house? I saw *Poltergeist*, and I don't want no damage... or no more than has already been done."

"What we do will depend on the ghost," Cooper answered, knowing this sounded cagey, but he couldn't offer more yet. "From what Lee has told me, neither of you has actually seen a spirit? There have just been objects moving through the air, and two of your pets were frozen while inside the house?"

Amy drew in a sharp breath and looked down at the table. "Poor Jewell and Sampson. Jewell had the sweetest singing voice, and Sampson..." She trailed off for a moment and her voice broke. "He was the smartest dog I ever knew."

Lee reached out and put his hand over hers. He was good at this type of comfort as it came to him naturally. "I'm sorry."

She gripped his hand but kept her eyes down.

Cooper looked to Mary. "We need to go to the house and figure out what we're dealing with. Lee said the issues didn't start until you broke through a locked door in the basement?"

"That's right." Mary nodded. "But there was almost nothing in the storage room, just some garden tools and a few boxes of junk. Like I said before, we haven't actually *seen* what could be causing all of this."

"There are a few methods to force a ghost to show itself," Cooper continued. "Once that happens, we'll be able to gauge its age. With new spirits, sometimes they just don't know they're dead, and I can help them cross over. With an older spirit, determined to stay and cause harm, it may need to be banished."

"And you can do that?"

"Yes, ma'am."

"Who taught you?"

He held her gaze. "My mother."

She sat for a long minute, watching him. Then she stood up walked to the counter, picked up a key, and came back. "I respect a man who learns from his mother." She handed him the key. "I hope you can solve this for us. We both fell in love with that old house."

This was the first time she'd sounded vulnerable, but it didn't stop him from answering, "We'll need half the payment up front and half on completion, and you'll need to sign the contract."

While he did believe they were helping people, this was business.

She nodded.

CHAPTER TWO:

THE GHOST

Pulling up outside an older house about ten miles outside of town, Cooper decided he could understand the attraction.

Perhaps the place hadn't come with much property, but the house was framed by maple trees on both sides. There was a remnant of what had once been a vegetable garden out front. The house itself was two stories, painted light blue with white trim. There were no other houses in sight. For someone wishing to live out of town with a bit of autonomy, this place would be worth a little renovation.

Lee barely glanced at the house as he got out of the Jeep. Instead, he opened one of the backseat doors and began rifling through a canvas pack. "What do you want to bring in? If this thing killed a dog, I vote for weapons... but maybe not the gas can or the blowtorch yet."

They always kept a gas can and a blowtorch in the back of the Jeep. Normally, when first scouting a possible haunting, they didn't bother with more than a few tire irons for protection—and rarely needed them. But here, Lee wasn't wrong.

"Yeah," Cooper agreed. "Load the gun and grab the bag with my onyx blade."

His mother had taught him how to use various crystals to repel spirits. Black tourmaline, onyx, and other agates all worked, but he preferred working with onyx. Lee preferred a shotgun loaded with rock-salt pellets.

he night they'd met, Lee had proven himself more than useful in a straight-up fight against a vampire. But he hadn't known anything about the spirit world until Cooper taught him. Still, he preferred to let Cooper handle the mystical side of the business—while he played defense or offense.

And as far as the mystical side went... Cooper couldn't help feeling conflicted. He came from two very different worlds and had never been able to reconcile the distance.

His mother's name was Katrina. She was a mix of a "free spirit" and a hard-headed businesswoman. She'd been raised in what she called "a hippie commune," and while she had respect for some things she'd learned from the people there, such as how to summon a ghost or how to read tarot cards with enough skill to earn money, she had nothing but contempt for her parents who she claimed were fools with no idea how to survive in a world without a grocery store. She had few good memories from childhood to share.

Cooper's father was of the Coastal Salish people, a descendent of the Shuswap tribe, and he had been a difficult man to know. Cooper's earliest memories stretched back to the age of three or four years old, while living in an apartment near Olympia, Washington.

He'd always felt invisible.

His mother had been wildly, deeply in love with his father. From what Cooper had observed, his father was incapable of loving anyone. He was a silent man, restless when indoors, and Cooper's mother spent every free moment trying to make him happy, trying to make him love her.

She'd never wanted children, but she'd had Cooper in the belief that somehow a family would make her husband settle down. She ran a side business as a psychic, reading tarot cards and using her "powers" to help people make decisions. She was good at what she did and earned enough for rent and groceries. From what Cooper could remember, his father hadn't earned a dime.

When Cooper was seven years old, his father moved them thirty miles from the nearest town, into a one-room shack in an isolated, heavily forested area. His father brought four rifles and began to spend his days hunting. Nearly half the time, he brought Cooper along, teaching his small son how to hunt and track. Sometimes they would fish instead.

They rarely spoke on these outings, but Cooper learned a good deal.

Upon their return to the shack, even at a young age, he felt embarrassment when his mother would come running out the door and cling to his father's neck desperately, as if they had been gone for weeks. Sometimes she would cry.

That was the worst, when she cried.

She hated living out in the forest, as there was no way for her to earn money, and food supplies were limited. This living arrangement reminded her too much of her youth. There was a bathroom with a toilet and a sink haphazardly built onto the back of the shack, but actual baths were taken in a steel tub. There was a woodstove for cooking—and heating water for baths.

Cooper and his father brought back deer, pheasant, and trout, but his mother was not skilled at boning fish or cooking wild game. His father cooked sometimes, but they often lived from large bags of dried beans and rice. Within six months, Cooper was dreaming of a McDonald's cheeseburger or Captain Crunch cereal with milk.

Months stretched into years.

Occasionally, they would drive his father's truck down into the nearest town to buy at least some supplies—and ammo for the rifles. His father made a little money selling dead animals he'd shot to a taxidermist, and later, Cooper learned that his mother had some savings. She may have hated their living situation, but she swore she would do anything to make his father happy.

She never once worried about whether Cooper was happy.

Sometimes, though, she did go through the motions of home-schooling him, and with books brought from their apartment, she taught him to read. With paper purchased at the grocery store, she taught him to write. She taught him basic math.

But by the time he was eleven, her savings were gone, and his father began going hunting alone, staying away for four or five days at a time. Cooper's mother would either pace in misery and agitation, or she would fall into sadness and sleep all day. Cooper learned to cook rice and beans, but he was so tired of them that on some days, he just went hungry.

Worse, each time his father returned, Cooper noted a wild look in his eyes—as if the man would rather not be at home. His father had stopped bathing or washing his clothes, and once, Cooper's mother referred to him as "going feral."

Cooper didn't know what this meant.

But somehow, even then, he knew that one day, his father would pick up a gun and leave and not come back.

About a month after Cooper's twelfth birthday, he woke up to find his father gone. Two of the rifles and all the remaining ammunition were gone.

"He's not coming back," Cooper told his mother.

She slapped him. Then she began to cry.

Had it been up to Cooper, they'd have packed their things into the truck that day and left the shack forever. They were almost out of food and had just enough gas to make it into town.

His mother made them wait three weeks.

Something shifted inside him in those three weeks. She watched him suffer from hunger and distress, and she didn't care. All she wanted was his father. She paced. She wept. She slept. Sometimes, she stood out-side the front door, like an abandoned dog, just waiting. But finally, at the end of three weeks, in despair, she helped him pack what was left of their belongings, and they left.

They coasted on fumes into the small town where they'd always bought groceries, and his mother begged a woman on the street to borrow her cell phone. Cooper wondered who she could be calling. But not long after, she brought him inside the grocery store, to the customer service desk. She showed her ID, signed a piece of paper, and the clerk handed her two hundred dollars in cash.

Cooper had never seen that much money.

"Your grandmother wired it to us," his mother said.

He'd never met a grandparent. "Your mother?"

"Money from my mother? God, no. Your father's mother. We're going to her now, but we won't stay long."

She bought them tuna sandwiches from the deli counter, chocolate chip cookies, and milk. They went back out to sit in the truck, and he ate like a starved wolf. The sandwich was a miracle, and he licked any remaining tuna from his fingers before starting on a cookie.

Then she filled up the tank and began to drive.

He didn't remember much about the journey to Quinault except that it didn't take more than a half a day. But he never forgot stepping out of the truck in front of a two-story log house and seeing a small, older woman with long black hair (streaked with white) coming to meet them.

She wore jeans and a wool shirt. Silver and turquoise earrings hung from her earlobes. The skin around her eyes was just beginning to crease. She walked straight to him and looked him up and down.

"You're Cooper?" she asked.

His mother just stood there. The two women did not address each other.

Wordless, Cooper nodded to the older woman.

"My name is Beatrice. You can call me Grandma Bea," she said. "Come on inside. I've got chili and cornbread on the stove. Your room is ready upstairs if you want to take up your things."

Chili, cornbread, and his own room? She said it so matter-of-factly. Something began melting inside him, and for the first time in his life, he experienced what it might be like to feel safe. By the time he went to bed that night, he never wanted to leave.

But true to her word, his mother began making arrangements to leave as soon as possible. They stayed two weeks, and in that time, Cooper grew to love his Grandma Bea. She was blunt and not physically affectionate, but in daily life, she put him first, and he loved her for it. She fixed him three meals a day. She bought him new jeans, T-shirts, socks, underwear, and sneakers.

In the downstairs bathroom of the cabin, there was a walk-in shower... with soap and shampoo.

She loaned them the money to lease a house down in Aberdeen (which seemed the size of a small city), and Cooper's mother went to work transforming the main living area into a mystic's "parlor." She bought used lamps and low couches. She bought a used round table with big chairs. She hung crystals, and she covered the lamps with sheer scarves. She bought herself new clothes.

Then she began advertising herself as a psychic.

Her client list grew quickly. Anyone who visited once always came back.

That year was the first time Cooper really *looked* at his mother.

She was not pretty in the traditional sense. Her nose was too large and her mouth too wide. Her eyes were set too far apart. Her face showed a few small pockmarks left over from teenage acne. But she had long, thick golden hair, bright blue eyes, and she now wore flowing dresses to play up the "mystic" element. When she was reading tarot cards, she could make the client across the table feel like the only person in the world. This was her gift.

Cooper never felt at home in this leased house, and he wanted to go back up to Quinault and stay with Grandma Bea, but his mother kept him in Aberdeen and enrolled him in school. He had to take some tests to get himself placed, but soon found himself in the Aberdeen middle school. After living in the wild for so long, he didn't fit in and had a difficult time relating to other people—or maybe they had a hard time relating to him.

Within a year, his mother had paid Grandma Bea back for the loan, and then she bought them a notebook computer. The computer fascinated Cooper, and he learned to use it quickly. His mother still had bad days where her addiction to his father took over, and she'd spend a day in bed weeping.

But most days she worked, and she became determined to teach him her skills—so that he might always have something to fall back on. When he started high school, she began branching out, posing as a medium who could commune with spirits, and sometimes they encountered real ghosts. This led to Cooper's first experiences with helping spirits cross over to the other side.

Nothing in his life had been normal, so he accepted the existence of ghosts in much the same way he accepted that his father had consciously chosen to walk into the woods one day and not come back.

But as a young man, Cooper nearly always felt lost, with no idea of his place in the world. He felt safe only during school breaks and summers when he was allowed to go and stay with Grandma Bea.

When he was eighteen, she suffered a sudden stroke and died. That was the first time he ever wept. In her will, she left him the log house and ten acres of land. It was paid for, but the property taxes were high, and for the first time, he had a purpose—to hang onto his grandmother's home. He left his mother, moved into the log house, and began taking on any paying work he could find.

Any work...

"Cooper!" Lee called, standing on the porch of the light blue house with white trim. "Are we going in or what?"

"I'm coming." Cooper walked up the steps toward the front door. "I've got the key."

But Lee reached out and opened the door. "It's not locked. They must have forgotten."

This wasn't surprising. When people left a house in a hurry, they often remembered doing things such as locking doors—when they had not. Mary wouldn't have bothered giving them the key unless she believed the place to be locked up.

Cooper followed Lee inside and looked around. He'd expected some damage, but he paused at the sight before them.

"Jesus Christ," Lee said, gripping the shotgun.

Glass from shattered lamps covered the floor. Framed family photos had been ripped from walls and broken into pieces. Chairs lay on the floor. Not a single knick-knack was intact. The living room looked as if someone wanted to destroy any remnant of the new occupants.

"I expect the kitchen may be worse," Lee said, leaning down over the torn image of a photo of Mary smiling with her arm around a little boy. "Whatever we're dealing with, it's angry."

"Stay here," Cooper answered. "Don't go in any farther yet."

Taking out his phone, he called Mary.

She answered on the first ring. "Yes?"

"It's Cooper," he said. "We're in the house. Last night, I was trying to learn about the history here, and I saw the place had been repossessed about six years ago. Do you know anything about that? Do know what happened?"

"No, but I never asked much. Our realtor might. Her name is Lisa Fischer. Do you want her number?"

"Yes. Text it to me right now."

They both hung up, and within a few seconds, a phone number came into his text messages. He called the number.

A cheerful voice answered, "Lisa Fischer."

"Hi Lisa," he said. "My name is Cooper Reyes. I'm working some security for Mary Faulkner in the house she bought outside of town. There have been a few incidents here."

"Incidents?" she repeated, sounding concerned. "What do you mean?"

"I can't disclose, but Mary gave me your number. This house was repossessed some time back. Do you know what happened?"

She paused for a few seconds. He waited.

"It was owned by a married couple, Garrett and Rachel Talbot," she said finally. "From what I understand, there were some... domestic problems. The police had been called in a few times and whatnot. Rachel was taken to the hospital once or twice. But then Garrett ran off, and Rachel couldn't make the mortgage payments on her own. It's unfortunate, but these things happen. I don't think the woman would cause Mary and Amy any trouble, though. The last I heard, she'd gone to live with her sister's family in Montana." She paused again. "You say you're handling a security issue?"

"Yes, but you'll need to speak with Mary or Amy for information. I'm not at liberty. Thank you for your help."

He hung up before she could ask more.

Lee stood watching him.

"Did you hear that?" Cooper asked.

"Yep. My guess is that Garrett didn't exactly run off."

Cooper could not disagree. "Let's find the stairs down to the basement."

"First, I'm going to get the gas can from the Jeep."

"No."

Lee's answering voice was firm. "Just in case."

.   .   .   .   .

Lee couldn't help feeling some trepidation as he descended the stairs into the basement and set down the gas can—while holding onto the shotgun. He didn't exactly mind hunting ghosts, but he preferred a more straight-up fight.

Or more to the point, he preferred working with Cooper in a straight-up fight. With vamps or were-wolves, there wasn't much room for moral ambiguity as it was usually an "us or them" situation. But ghosts were different, and Cooper couldn't help being who he was. Lee wouldn't haven't wanted to change him.

There were three basic ways that Cooper handled a ghost. His preferred method was to make contact, communicate with the spirit, and help it understand that it needed to cross over. More than half the time, this worked.

When it didn't, they switched to the second method, which was to use several weapons (such as the onyx crystal blade and the shotgun) to drive it from the house or place of haunting. Ghosts were normally so shocked by anything that could actually hurt them, they would flee. Cooper could then quickly ward the house against re-entry. At first, the spirit would panic and scream and attempt to get back in. But after spending a few hours—sometimes a few days—out in the world, once Cooper tried to communicate with them again, this time, they would listen and let him help them cross.

The third method was a last resort, and in all the ghosts they'd hunted together, they'd used it only twice.

If a spirit was determined to remain, and no amount of reason seemed to get through, and it was a clear danger to the living, Cooper would make the decision to banish. They'd find the person's bones or something to which it was strongly connected, pour gasoline, light the bones or object on fire, and Cooper would use a banishing incantation.

Apparently, his mother had taught him to do this, but she'd drilled into his head (maybe a little too much) that such measures should be rare, used only in ex-treme circumstances. She said a very small percentage of ghosts were harmful, but that if a vengeful spirit was destroyed in this fashion, there was no telling what happened to the soul.

As a result, Cooper had put himself—and Lee—into danger more than once trying to avoid this third option. He didn't like the idea of destroying a soul. Of course, Lee didn't blame him. It was just that Lee put his own safety, and Cooper's, first.

In the basement, both men looked around. With the exception of a few stacks of boxes, it appeared empty. But Lee could smell mold.

"There's the broken door," Cooper said, starting across the room.

Lee cut him off and pushed open the door first. It looked like Mary Faulkner had used something solid to break the handle. Upon stepping inside the storage room, he saw the garden tools she had mentioned and more boxes and...

"Coop," he said, pointing with his free hand.

Across the storage room, he saw a small, half-open door to what was probably a closet. Someone had painted a large white symbol on the door, a circle with a tree in the middle. Seven branches from the tree stretched to the outside edges of the circle, becoming part of it.

"Looks like you aren't the only one with a little knowledge," Lee added. "You recognize the ward?"

Cooper took a quick breath and walked to the closet door. "It's a binding ward." He touched a broken padlock. "Mary must have forced this open after breaking into the storage room. But she didn't mention it."

"Probably didn't think it mattered."

Cooper opened the closet door and looked inside. "It's empty."

He stepped inside, and Lee went to join him, standing in the closet doorway while Cooper softly rapped on the back wall of the closet.

"False back," he said without sounding surprised.

Using both hands, he pushed against the wall. It gave inward slightly and then popped open. Cooper stepped back, and Lee looked down. He already knew what they'd find, but it still made him wince. A desiccated body leaned against the wall. From the look of the corpse, he had been a large man with a head full of reddish hair. He wore boots, overalls, and what may have been a T-shirt.

There was a hole in his chest the size of Lee's fist.

"I suspect he sent Rachel to the hospital one too many times," Lee mused.

Cooper glanced back toward the door. "Yeah. She probably shot him in another room and somehow dragged him in here and hid his body behind the false back. She warded the door and padlocked it. Then she locked the storage room."

Foolish on some levels. Had she really believed no one would ever find the body?

"Why the ward?" Lee asked. "How could she have worried he'd come back as a ghost?"

Cooper shook his head. "Maybe she thought he was too mean to die."

Lee couldn't help feeling sorry for the woman, who had most likely been defending herself. Still, leaving her husband might have been a better option than shooting him. Then again, maybe he wouldn't let her leave.

"It's been dead quiet in the house since we arrived," he said. "You going to summon him right away?"

Crouching down, Cooper took a jackknife from his jacket pocket, opened it, and cut off a few strands of hair from the corpse's head. Just as he turned to answer Lee, a fierce wind blew through the storage room, slamming the room's door shut.

Their gear was on the other side, out in the main basement.

.　　.　　.　　.

Cooper ran for the door.

To his relief, when he jerked on it, it opened. The wind was blowing out here now, and he dove for his pack, pulling out his onyx blade first. He'd had this made to order. The entire weapon was about sixteen inches long, with a polished wooden handle.

But he set the blade down quickly, grabbed a piece of

chalk, and drew a circle around himself. Neither the chalk nor the circle themselves held any kind of magical properties, but while he was casting, the spellcraft allowed him to use the circle as a barrier from anything entering the small space inside.

Then he took out a clear quartz crystal, a brass bowl, a small knife, and a lighter. After setting the crystal in the center of the bowl, he put in the strands of Garrett's hair. Cutting the index finger of his left hand, he let a few drops of blood drip down onto the hair. There were several variations of this spell—as he didn't always have access to the body. But using something of the person's corpse was fastest and most effective.

Then he lit the hair on fire, crossed his legs, and closed his eyes.

"*Spiritus, ostende mihi te ipsum,*" he whispered.

He didn't need to look backwards to know Lee was standing right behind him, inside the circle, with the shotgun.

Focusing his energy on the spirit's presence in the house, Cooper raised his voice louder, calling out, "*Spiritus, ostende mihi te ipsum!*"

He opened his eyes.

The air in front him shimmered and wavered. Then a transparent form appeared. It was Garrett. As his desiccated corpse suggested, he'd been a large man, well over six feet, with heavy muscles that were just going to fat. He appeared in the same clothes he'd died in, the overalls and T-shirt. The hole in his chest was visible, looking exactly as the day it had happened, with blood soaking the bib of his overalls.

Cooper was looking straight at him; Garrett's face shifted into a mask of rage as he realized they could see him. His form whooshed to the edge of the circle, and he screamed, the sound so loud it hurt Cooper's ears. Garrett's lips were curled back over yellowed teeth as anger poured out of his mouth in one long enraged cry. At present, he posed no danger, though, as he couldn't cross the circle.

Cooper got up onto his knees.

"Garrett, listen to me!" he called. "Listen. You are dead, but your spirit is still here. You need to cross over to find peace."

"Where is she?" Garrett shouted. "Where is that bitch?"

He was looking around wildly, and Cooper didn't know if he was referring to his wife, Rachel... or to Mary or Amy. The men he'd known who reminded him of Garrett often referred to most women by names like bitch.

"I'll kill her!" Garrett said.

Still inside the circle, Lee stepped up beside Cooper, leveled the shotgun at Garrett and spoke for the first time.

"You need to calm down," he said. "Believe it or not, we're trying to help you."

Focusing on Lee, Garrett's transparent face twisted into an expression of madness. He didn't even seem to see the gun. With no warning, one of the boxes stacked against the wall flew off the top of the stack and smashed into Lee. Unprepared, he stumbled backward, outside the circle.

Garrett struck instantly, flying the few feet between them and straight into Lee's body.

"Lee!" Cooper called, scrambling to his feet.

His friend's eyes went wide as he dropped the shotgun and began turning pale, clutching himself as his teeth chattered. This was the main threat from an angry spirit: the cold. Garrett could freeze Lee to death in a matter of minutes.

Cooper rushed outside the circle, grabbed Lee's head and pressed the flat of the onyx blade against the side of his face. With a whooshing sound, Garrett flew from Lee's body, crying out from pain and shock. The blade couldn't truly injure him, but the touch of it would hurt.

Dropping the blade, Cooper picked up the shotgun, aimed and fired. The transparent image of Garrett's body shattered, but this would buy them only a few seconds. With his free hand, he grabbed Lee's upper arm and tried to drag him back inside the circle.

Garrett materialized again, and this time, he flew straight into Cooper.

. . . . .

Lee was so cold.

His lungs felt like they'd been turned to ice as he tried to suck in air. He could still feel remnants from Garrett's madness and rage crawling around inside his brain. He could barely move his near-frozen arms. He'd experienced few things in their profession worse than having his body invaded by a ghost.

But in the split second that he saw Cooper fall, turning pale and gasping for breath, he made a decision on his own.

He had only moments to act.

Somehow, he got to his feet and started running toward the stairs for the gas can. The second he picked it up, he whirled and ran back, going through the circle, whisking the lighter off the floor without pausing.

He rushed to the storage room, to the closet. Then he splashed gasoline over Garrett's corpse, clicked the lighter, and dropped it. Garrett's dead body ignited.

Without even hesitating, Lee ran back to the main basement. Cooper was doubled over on the floor, his eyes opened in pain, his face turning blue. Lee grabbed the onyx blade. This time, he pressed it to Cooper's face, and Garrett flew out. But now, the ghost appeared confused, looking toward the storage room.

Lee propped Cooper into a sitting position. "Now!" he yelled. "You have to do it now!"

Cooper choked a few times attempting to breathe. Garrett turned back toward them, his confusion turning to anger.

A few unintelligible words escaped from Cooper's mouth. But he managed to take a breath.

"Now!" Lee shouted again.

"*Ad quos eieci te de hoc planum esse videatur,*" Cooper said, and after drawing in a deeper breath, his voice strengthened. *"Et ultra non faciam nocere."*

Garrett's transparent body hung in the air, as if he couldn't move. The anger on his face shifted to fear as he tried to fly forward.

Cooper struggled up to his feet, still weak, but he called out clearly, *"Ad quos eieci te de hoc planum esse videatur! Et ultra non faciam nocere!"*

The air shimmered and wavered again. Garrett clawed and thrashed as he began to fade. Cooper dropped to his knees, as if unable to remain standing.

Still thrashing, the spirit of Garrett faded and faded... and disappeared.

He was gone.

Smoke was coming from the storage room, and Lee ran, ripping off his jacket as he moved. Upon reaching the closet, he saw that Garrett's corpse had been burned down to blackened remnants of bone, but this was enough. Something about the combination of the fire and the incantation happening at the same time worked to banish a spirit.

As quickly as he could, Lee used his heavy canvas jacket to beat out the fire. It wouldn't do to burn Mary and Amy's house down now that Garrett was permanently gone. When he was satisfied the fire was completely out, he walked back out to find Cooper still kneeling on the floor with his arms crossed, attempting to recover.

Lee wasn't sure what to say and anxiety rose inside him. Banishing a spirit was always Cooper's decision—not his.

"I didn't see a choice," he said finally.

"There was no choice," Cooper answered, barely loud enough to be heard. "You did the only thing you could."

Although he already knew this to be true, Lee couldn't help the relief. There would be no repercussions from him taking matters into his own hands.

He needed this job.

He needed a home.

He needed this friendship.

CHAPTER THREE:

THE NEST

March passed into April.

The Quinault rainforest wasn't called a rainforest for nothing, but there were fair days in the spring too. When not out on a job, Cooper and Lee had plenty to do at home. Lee always seemed to be working on his truck, and Cooper handled their bookkeeping or updating the website.

There was wood to cut and split.

Some days, they'd go to the river and spend a day fishing.

Neither of them was much of a cook, so they tended to eat a good deal of canned soup or canned chili—and a lot of sandwiches—but they got by. At night, they would normally drink a few beers and watch TV or maybe a movie on the DVD player, as they had quite a collection. Every Sunday, they played poker to see who had to clean the bathrooms. Cooper was well aware that most people would find their home life less than exciting, but it suited the two of them. He slept in the master bedroom downstairs, and Lee had taken the largest bedroom upstairs. They used the other two bedrooms for storage.

Since the trip to Idaho in March, they'd handled two more ghost hunts, but nothing on the level of having to banish Garrett Talbot. In both cases, Cooper was able to help the spirits cross over. He still felt regret over Garrett, but Lee *had* done the right thing. Garrett had been

both beyond reason and a danger to the living. Sometimes, Cooper still shuddered from memories of the
madness he'd felt when Garrett had entered him.

This was an occupational hazard.

But after telling Mary Faulkner and Amy the story of
what happened, they'd left matters up to the women.
There was a burned corpse in their basement, and it was
up to them if they wanted to report it to the police or not.

Upon collecting the second half of their payment,
Cooper and Lee had driven back to Quinault. This was
their policy. They handled the hunting, but once it was
done, *they* were done. Any fallout was left to the client.
That's what the signed contract was for.

In the second week of April, Cooper spent a morning
fishing. He caught three trout. Once back home, he put
them into the fridge. As the cupboards in the kitchen
were somewhat bare, a run into Aberdeen for groceries
seemed in order. He was just about to see if Lee wanted
to come with him—and maybe grab a hamburger at the
diner for lunch—when the business cell rang.

"Permanent Solutions Unnatural," he answered. "How
can I help you?"

"Cooper?"

The male voice was vaguely familiar, but he couldn't
place it.

"I don't know if you'll remember me," the man said.
"I'm the sheriff from Mason Creek, Oregon. You and
Lee did... a job for me last year."

At this prompt, Cooper remembered the man well,
Damon Tucker. He'd been smart enough to realize there
was something unnatural about a killer his small department was hunting, and he'd contacted Cooper. The
end result had been Lee taking the head off a vampire.

"Yes, Sheriff. It's good to hear from you. Everything
okay?"

This was just good manners. Clearly things were not
okay—or the man wouldn't be calling.

"I'm... we're having some trouble again, only worse
this time."

"How much worse?"

"I got three bodies in the morgue, torn up and drained of blood, and two missing persons all in just over a week."

"One week?"

That was unusual. Most vampires fed only two or three times a month—and they kept a low profile.

"I don't want to get my men involved," Sheriff Tucker said. "They still don't know the truth about that business last year. Would you and Lee come down? I can give you better details once you're here."

"Yes. We'll be at the station by ten o'clock tomorrow morning."

"Thanks. I mean it."

Cooper hung up.

He walked outside to the carport to find Lee working on his old Ford pickup, with tools spread all over the concrete floor.

"Pack it in," Cooper said. "We got a job."

.   .   .   .   .

It was about a seven-hour drive from their home down to Mason Creek in southern Oregon, but they took time to prepare first. A vampire hunt was different from a ghost hunt. Cooper checked the flashlights they'd put together with sunlamp bulbs.

Lee packed two handguns, the shotgun, and two machetes.

Contrary to mythology, vampires didn't explode in sunlight, and when necessary, they could walk around outside on a cloudy day. But in direct contact, sunlight could burn their skin enough to startle or slow them down. Holy water or a stake through the heart were also myths. The only methods Cooper had found to kill one were to take its head off or burn it completely. A bullet wouldn't kill a vampire, but Cooper tended to hunt with a gun in one hand and a machete in the other. If he shot a vampire in the kneecap, it went down like anything else.

Leaving Quinault about one o'clock in the afternoon, they made good time down Interstate 5 and even got through Portland without too much traffic (which could be a nightmare in rush hour). Then they started the long drive south to Mason Creek.

Even after a stop for a quick meal in Eugene, they arrived about eight o'clock that night. Cooper found a Motel 6 and got them a room. They'd barely walked in the door and set their bags down when Lee said, "I'm going out, see if I can find a bar."

Cooper was used to staying in motels by himself while on hunts. Lee never dated at home, as he didn't care to be shopping in the cereal aisle at Safeway and run into someone he'd slept with. So he viewed their trips away as an opportunity for this side of his recreational needs.

Tonight, for once, Cooper found himself wanting to go out as well, but he didn't suggest it. Lee wasn't the type to need a wing man; he preferred picking up women alone.

"Okay," Cooper said. "I'll research the local news here and see what I learn. Just remember the sheriff's expecting us by ten."

"We'll be there," Lee called, walking out the door.

.   .   .   .   .

In downtown Mason Creek, Lee walked into a dimly lit bar called Smokey Jay's on the north end of Main Street. There was no actual smoke inside—as no one was allowed to smoke within twenty feet of the entrance. But the name somehow appealed to him.

Plus, the place was fairly crowded for a Thursday night. There were two pool tables in the back and a dart board on the west wall. It was his kind of place. In a matter of seconds, he'd scanned the entire room. Most people sat in groups. There were a few women sitting alone at tables, but he discounted them instantly.

Women sitting alone at a table tended to want to be left alone, and he wasn't a man to intrude. The art of seduction or "the chase" had never appealed to Lee. He did enough hunting in his professional life. Having to somehow convince a woman to sleep with him was also a foreign—and unappealing—concept.

For him, sex only worked if the woman wanted him and she made it clear. He liked being wanted. Fortunately, he'd been born with a physical "look" that appealed to most women. He also possessed an easygoing energy, and he was a good listener. This combination served him well.

Turning away from the numerous tables, he looked toward the bar.

A woman sitting alone at a bar, with an innocuous empty stool beside her, was normally looking for company. His gaze landed on an auburn-haired woman sitting alone, drinking a glass of white wine. The stools on both sides of her were empty.

Walking over, he sat down. There was a limited food menu on the wall behind the bar.

"I was just about to order a plate of nachos," he said to her. "Have you eaten dinner?"

While such an opening might not have worked for all men, his Southern accent made it sound like a friendly invitation. Swiveling her head toward him, she looked up into his face.

He wavered.

She was young, maybe twenty-two, wearing jeans, a pink T-shirt, and sandals. Her hair was pulled back into a ponytail, with long bangs tucked behind her ears. She wore no makeup but sported a small gold hoop in each earlobe. She didn't look like a girl who hung out in bars, sitting alone on a stool.

"I..." she started to answer. Her expression was a little lost. "I..."

The bartender came over. "What can I get you?" he asked Lee.

"Darkest beer you have on tap," Lee answered. Then he asked the girl, "What do you think about those nachos?"

She nodded. "Yes. I did miss dinner."

Lee smiled at the bartender. "One plate of nachos. Make it a large." As the bartender headed off, Lee turned back to the girl. "My name's Lee."

"Nicole Summers," she answered quietly.

"You all right?" He meant the question. He wanted an answer, and she responded to his honest interest.

"It's been a hard week," she said. "My brother, Nathan, went missing."

That kicked his hesitation instincts even further into overload. Cooper had mentioned there were three corpses and two people missing. By bad luck, he could be sitting with someone connected to the job they were about to undertake. Lee wasn't fond of connections.

"Missing?" he asked. "You don't think he's just gone off for some fun? Forgot to let anyone know?"

"No." She shook her head. "We have family plans every Sunday. Nathan never misses Sunday dinner. But he went out Saturday night, and no one has seen or heard from him since."

"Went out?"

"He came here."

The bartender set down Lee's beer, and Nicole looked all around herself at the bar. "I've never been here. I don't come to places like this. But it was the last place anyone saw him."

Women—and men—often said they didn't come to places like this, but in Nicole's case, Lee knew it was the truth. Also, she'd just given him a useful piece of infor-mation. If her brother was one of the missing persons, and the last place anyone had seen him was in this bar, that could give Lee and Cooper a place to start.

"You close to your brother?" he asked.

She'd barely touched her wine. "Not so much. He's ten years older than me. But he's my brother, and my family is so upset. The police haven't learned anything to help."

The bartender set down a plate of nachos with ground beef, cheese, black olives, green onions, and sour cream.

"Eat something," Lee said to Nicole.

Quickly, she ate two of the nachos, and then she seemed to come back to herself, looking at him again. "I don't even know you. I don't know why I'm telling you all this."

"'Cause I'm listening."

He drank some of his beer, and they ate the nachos together. But he was uncertain about taking this any further. She was vulnerable, and he was not one to take advantage. She also struck him as the type who slept only with a boyfriend, and he was no one's boyfriend. Watching the stream of men who had married or lived with his mother had taught him the damage of relationships. The only tie he wanted was to Cooper, and in many ways (the important ways), Cooper was a lot like him.

Cooper wanted no other ties either, not even a house cat. Cooper never brought home strays, and he never took responsibility for anyone besides himself and Lee. This ensured that their home remained reliable and stable. Cooper's own mother still lived in Aberdeen, and they rarely saw her.

This was part of the reason their friendship, their partnership, worked.

"I just wish the police could tell us something," Nicole said, "even if it's bad news. At least we'd know."

"They will. It may take some time, but they'll figure out what's happened."

"You think?"

"Yes."

She exhaled in what sounded like relief. On her barstool, she half-turned her body toward his and ran her eyes over his face. He was surprised to see a familiar expression. She wanted him. He'd seen that look more times than he could remember.

But he was still cautious. "I'm just passing through town with a friend. He and I will be gone in a day or two." He wanted no illusions here and let his words sink in. "And I can see you're worrying about your brother. I don't want to intrude. Would you rather be alone?"

With her eyes still on his face, she shook her head. "No. I don't want to be alone. I don't want to be alone at all."

. . . . .

The next morning, at nine-thirty, Cooper was standing outside a motel room again when Lee pulled up in the Jeep.

This was a familiar scene for them both, but Cooper walked around to the driver's side. "Why don't you let me drive? Sheriff Tucker called this morning. Another body came in last night, and he asked us to meet him at the morgue instead the station. I've got the address."

Lee appeared distracted, his gaze drifting down the street. "Mmmmmm?"

"I'll drive."

Lee turned the Jeep off, got out, and helped Cooper pack up their gear and bags. They never left guns in the Jeep at night. Then Cooper got in the driver's side. As he watched Lee climb in and reach for the passenger side seat belt, he frowned.

"What's wrong?"

"Mmmmmmm?" Lee asked again.

"You just look..." Cooper couldn't think of the right word. Troubled? "I don't know, but something's wrong. Did you have a rough night?"

"No, it was nice. But the girl wasn't my usual type, and I'm thinking I should have walked out of the bar and come back to the motel."

It took a few seconds for Cooper to recognize the odd quality in Lee's voice. "Is that guilt?" he asked. "Are you feeling guilty?"

"What?" Lee snapped, turning toward him. "Hell no. I just... I've got a bad feeling her brother is one of the missing persons we're going to be looking into today. She was a bit low last night, and I should have walked out. I shouldn't have gone home with her."

"Her brother?"

"Yeah. She said we were sitting in the last place he'd been seen, a bar downtown called Smokey Jay's."

Cooper mulled that over. It wasn't like Lee to get involved with anyone connected to a hunt. But if this girl's brother was one of the missing people on Sheriff Tucker's list, then Cooper would go check out the bar himself.

Lee fell silent, and Cooper started the Jeep.

Since the entire town of Mason Creek comprised about three square miles, it didn't take long for Cooper to locate the address he'd been given. Though the sheriff had used the word "morgue," that wasn't exactly accurate. The closest hospital was in Roseburg, but Mason Creek boasted a large medical center, and apparently, the newest body had been taken there.

Cooper parked the Jeep, and then he and Lee entered the center through the back doors.

Just down the hallway, a short, muscular man in a uniform was pacing impatiently. His dark hair was going gray at the temples.

"Sheriff," Cooper called.

When the man turned, his relief was visible. He strode forward and shook both Cooper and Lee's hand, in turn, with a firm grip.

"Thank you for coming," he said briskly. "This is a bad business. With four bodies, I'm expecting the feds to arrive any time now, and I'd like to get a handle on this." Immediately, he turned and walked through an open doorway. "In here."

Inside a small room, Cooper saw a covered body on a steel table.

"She'll be transported to Roseburg soon, but I wanted you to have a look first," the sheriff said.

"She?" Lee asked.

"Yes. All four victims have been women, but both of the missing persons are men."

Cooper went over and pulled the cover off the body. The sight of dead bodies had never bothered him. At that point, the body was only a shell. Though he felt pity at the sight, he was not shocked. He'd seen a number of bodies in a similar condition. This woman looked to be in her mid-twenties with shoulder-length, blond hair. Her neck and wrists were torn open, leaving jagged, gaping wounds.

Lee walked to the other side of the table. His expression was unreadable.

"We don't have an ID yet," the sheriff said.

"Where was she found?" Lee asked.

"In an alley, just off Main Street."

Lee looked up. "North end or south end?"

"North. Why?"

"No reason." Lee paused. "I met a girl in town last night, named Nicole Summers. Is her brother, Nathan, one of the missing men on your list?"

"He is. No one has seen him since last Saturday." Suddenly, the sheriff appeared frustrated. "But this is just like before, right? You think we're hunting something like... whatever the hell that thing was."

"Yes," Cooper answered. "We'll take care of it." He stepped back. "But this may take us a few days."

The sheriff understood what he was saying and answered, "I've got a discretionary fund at my disposal. You work up a bid and I'll pay it."

"Good enough."

.   .   .   .   .

For Lee, the afternoon passed slowly, which wasn't a good thing. His mind was busy, and he'd never been fond of a busy mind.

He and Cooper drove down to the police station to meet up again with Sheriff Tucker. They handled the contract and payment agreement first. Then the sheriff shared everything he knew about the murder victims and missing people, which wasn't much. He gave them files with copies of photographs of the two missing men—provided by their families.

But Lee wasn't worried. He already knew where and how they'd start looking for answers. Still, he couldn't get Nicole Summers off his mind. She'd been kind to him last night, taken him home to her small apartment, slept with him, and then made him buttered toast, coffee and orange juice for breakfast. Things like a woman making him breakfast affected him more than he cared to admit. Plus, he could see she was lonely, and he wouldn't even have considered giving her his phone number.

He felt bad.

And normally, he never felt bad after a night with a woman when out on the road. But he also normally followed his instincts and only hooked up with women who were just like him. Still, there was one thing he could do for Nicole, and that was to find out what had happened to her brother.

That much, he *could* do for her.

By the time they left the sheriff's station, it was mid-afternoon. They stopped at a Subway drive-through to pick up few sandwiches and then headed back to their room. For a Motel 6, their room was fairly comfortable. The motel was advertised as a place for "extended stays," so the room came with a small kitchen, a full-sized couch, two queen-sized beds, and plenty of clean towels in the bathroom.

There was also a desk for Cooper's computer, and he fired it up to look at maps of the outlying areas.

"You think we're dealing with a nest, don't you?" Lee asked, sitting on one of the beds.

"Maybe. Probably. What bothers me is a body just left lying in an alley. Vamps are usually better at keeping under the radar. So, it's either a nest and one of them doesn't know to be careful... or some vampire has lost its reason and is killing for the sake of killing."

Lee considered this while eating his roast beef sandwich.

When he finished, he tossed the wrapper and then lay down on the bed. "I didn't get much sleep. I think I'll nap until it's time to go."

"How soon can we head over?"

"About seven. The regulars always start coming around seven."

He closed his eyes.

At seven-fifteen that night, Lee and Cooper found an open parking spot right in front of Smokey Jay's, and they both went inside. On a Friday night, the place was already starting to get busy. Lee scanned the room again, this time actively looking for people sitting alone at tables.

But he didn't speak to anyone yet and just followed Cooper to the bar. The same bartender from last night was mixing drinks. He was in his early thirties, with a slight build, wearing a Foo Fighters T-shirt.

As they approached the bar, he recognized Lee.

"Dark beer and nachos?" he asked.

Lee smiled. "Good memory, but I'll just have the beer tonight, and one for my friend."

Cooper sat on a stool while looking around the place. Lee knew he was taking stock of doors, hallways, and exits.

When the bartender returned with their beers, Cooper said, "We're working some private investigations for Sheriff Tucker." He laid down two photographs, including one of Nathan Summers. "Do you mind if I ask you about these men?"

Nathan resembled Nicole in coloring, with thick, auburn hair and a healthy complexion.

"Private investigations?" the bartender repeated. But he didn't seem anxious or offended. "The sheriff was in a few days ago. I told him everything I could, but I wasn't much help."

Lee already knew this. So did Cooper. Sheriff Tucker had told them about everyone he'd questioned.

But they weren't only here to speak to the bartender.

Cooper continued asking the man questions about the two men in the photos as Lee turned away from them and studied the room. He saw an older woman sitting alone, but she appeared drunk. There was a man with a grizzled face sitting alone who looked like a regular as well, but he was clearly not paying attention to anything going on around him as he stared into a half-empty glass of beer. Then... Lee spotted a woman in her late forties with dyed red hair, sitting alone by the front windows of the place, drinking what appeared to be vodka and tonic. Though she sipped it slowly, her glass was nearly empty. But she wasn't drunk. Her eyes followed the people walking past her table. She also had a good view of the street.

She was his best bet.

Through some of their jobs, he'd gained a bit of knowledge about police procedure, and for all the buzz about DNA and scientific evidence, he'd learned that most information was gleaned from talking to people. He just had to find the right people.

Walking to the table, he smiled down at her.

"You ready for another?" he asked.

Without responding, she watched him cautiously, but he signaled to a waitress walking past them. The waitress nodded and headed for the bar.

Lee sat down at the table. The red-haired woman was still watching him. She wore a good deal of makeup, and the roots of her red hair were gray.

"You were here last night," she said. "Left with some little thing barely old enough to drink."

As he leaned back, his smiled broadened. "You have a good memory."

"It's not hard to notice you."

"I'll take that as a compliment."

The waitress came over with a vodka tonic. She set it down and whisked off again.

"Why are you buying me a drink?" the woman asked. "I clearly ain't your type. I got more mileage on me than that Jeep you pulled up in."

She'd noticed their rig when they parked. Although this was a good sign for his purposes, it also brought sympathy rising up inside him. She must be completely alone to be sitting here watching the world around her that carefully.

"I'm working a job," he said. "And that 'little thing' I left with last night is missing a brother."

The sheriff had given him and Cooper each their own set of photos, and he laid a file on the table, opening it to expose an image of Nathan Summers. "Did you see him in here last Saturday night?"

She didn't even glance down at the photo but kept her gaze on him. "You a cop? You don't look like a cop."

"No, ma'am. I'm more of a private investigator, but I'd be glad to pay you for anything you can remember about the man in this photo." He gently pushed Nathan's photo off the top, exposing a second photo of a man in his late twenties, the other missing person. He had white-blond hair and full-sleeved tattoos up both arms. "Or this one. His name's Quinn Moore. His mother filed the missing person's report last week."

"Pay me?" That got her attention, and this time, she looked down at the pictures and back up again. "How much?"

Lee was used to paying for information. Sometimes, they even billed this to the client. He had a feeling she wouldn't go cheap. Taking a hundred dollars in cash from his wallet, he slid it across the table.

"I'd appreciate anything you can remember."

After taking a long sip of her drink, she reached out, picked up the money, and said, "Yeah, they've both been here. They left with the cowboy."

"The cowboy?"

"That's what we call him, tall guy, always wearing a brown cowboy hat."

Lee didn't miss the term "we," but he ignored it for now. "Can you tell me any more about this cowboy, what he drives, where he lives?"

Turning her head, she looked to the grizzled man who'd been staring into his beer. He was watching them both now. "Charles," she said. "Come over and sit."

Without hesitation, the man came over to sit beside her. "What you got going, Nita?"

"The man here is paying money for information." She pointed down to the two photographs. "Tell him what you told me about the cowboy and that Sweetwater cabin."

Charles looked expectantly at Lee. But Lee could see he'd go cheaper than Nita, so he passed two twenties across the table.

Charles grabbed the money quickly. "I was out trying to get me some fish early Wednesday morning, just before sunrise, and I seen the cowboy and some others squatting in the old cabin near the creek."

"Squatting?" Lee asked.

"You know, staying there when it ain't theirs. That place has been abandoned for years, but Miles Johnson still owns the land."

This was useful. Clearly, the sheriff hadn't spoken with these two. But police rarely thought to speak with the local town drunks.

"How many people did you see there?"

"Hard to say. Three or four on the porch, but there could have been more inside."

This sounded like a nest. Lee had only dealt with a few, but some vampires didn't like being alone.

"Can you tell me how to get to this cabin?" he asked.

When Charles looked at him expectantly again, Lee almost smiled. These two were shaking him down. He pushed over another twenty.

"Just take the Days Creek Cutoff Road about seven miles southeast out of town," Charles said. "Turn left onto Sweetwater. You'll see it."

"Thank you," Lee said, standing. "I appreciate the help."

He walked back to the bar to find Cooper sitting alone, sipping his beer.

"Anything?" Cooper asked.

"Maybe. Cost me a hundred and sixty bucks, but I might have something."

"We'll expense it. Where are we going?"

"About seven miles out of town."

· · · · ·

Cooper drove, following Lee's instructions. He pulled over and parked the Jeep when they reached a narrow road called Sweetwater. It was fully dark outside, with a half-moon visible above the trees. Lee had shared what little he'd learned on the drive over, but if they were dealing with a nest, Cooper didn't want anyone seeing their headlights.

Both of them got out and started to gear up, each stuffing a sunlamp flashlight into their jacket pockets and double-checking to make sure the guns were properly loaded. They each took a handgun and a machete, leaving the shotgun behind this time. They'd need to move quickly once the fight started, and the guns were mainly used for injuring or slowing something down.

Cooper had no qualms about killing vampires. He'd been doing this long enough to know that the person—whoever he or she had been—died at the moment of being turned. He had no idea what happened to their souls, but just like the body at the medical center, all that was left was a shell.

He viewed himself as putting down a dangerous shell.

"You ready?" Lee whispered.

"Yep."

Cooper led the way into the dense trees. They hadn't gone more than hundred feet when he saw light up ahead, and they crept to the edge of the tree line to see an old cabin with a moss-covered roof. There was a decaying porch and large front windows. But one of the windows was cracked and the other was missing a pane.

Someone inside the cabin was shouting.

"God dammit, Quinn! I told you to be careful."

Silently, Cooper crossed the small open space between the tree line and cabin, and he stepped up onto the porch, dropping low and creeping forward until he could just see through the window without a pane. He needed to know what they were facing. Lee followed but didn't get up onto the porch.

Peering inside, Cooper could see four men, all standing, and what appeared to be a girl, crouched in a corner with her face hidden in her hands. He recognized Nathan Summers and Quinn Moore from their photos. The third man was muscular with a shaved head. He appeared to be in his mid-fifties, by far the oldest of the group. The fourth man was the one shouting. He was tall and looked to be about thirty-five, wearing a brown cowboy hat. His face was narrow, and even from where Cooper crouched, he could see the man's eyes were a vivid shade of light green.

Any light inside was provided by oil lamps, leaving Cooper to assume there was no electricity.

"That girl was found in an alley right downtown!" the man in the hat was shouting. "Two blocks from the bar. That's the fourth body you've left just lying on the ground. We're going to have to move states now."

"I didn't kill her!" Quinn shouted back. "It wasn't me this time. Burke, it wasn't me."

He looked just like his photo, white-blond hair glowing by lamplight and blue ink running up both arms. He'd called the man in the hat Burke.

"Well it wasn't James," Burke said, pointing to the older man with the shaved head. "He's not stupid." He turned to Nathan. "Nathan? Did you leave that girl in the alley?"

There was no answer at first, and then Nathan let out a hissing sound. His upper lip curled back, exposing fangs. "I was hungry."

Burke started toward him with a snarl, but Cooper had heard enough.

All four men were vampires. Nathan and Quinn had both been turned.

Creeping backward off the porch, he whispered to Lee, "There are four inside. The one in the hat seems to be the leader. Take him out first. Both Nathan and Quinn are new, less than two weeks turned. They shouldn't be much trouble. There's an older one who hasn't said anything, but he's one of them. There's a girl crouched in a corner. I don't know about her."

Lee nodded. "Wait here." He vanished around the back of the cabin and returned quickly. "There's a back door. I'll go in through there. You take the front. Just wait for the sound and then go in."

Cooper nodded, and Lee vanished again.

After crawling beneath the window, Cooper stood directly in front of the closed front door, gun in one hand, machete in the other. He didn't have to wait long. Within moments, the sound of splintering wood and a loud crash rang out, followed by a gunshot.

Cooper kicked in the front door. He saw Burke down on one knee—his other kneecap a bloody mess. Lee rushed and swung hard, taking Burke's head off in the first sweep. Blackish blood sprayed out, and Burke's body hit the floor. Cutting through a man's spinal column took greater than average strength, even with a sharp blade. Cooper considered himself strong, but he rarely made it with one swing.

Lee rarely needed two.

They had the element of surprise, but at the sight of Burke's head coming off, all three other vampires flew into motion. James, the older man with the shaved head, rushed Lee. Quinn and Nathan both ran for the back door.

Cooper shot Nathan in the right leg, causing him to fall. Then as Cooper ran past, he fired a second bullet into Nathan's head.

Quinn made it out the door.

Cooper raced outside after him, pausing long enough to aim the gun and shoot him between the shoulder blades. Quinn stumbled but didn't go down. Near the tree line, Cooper caught up with him as he turned to fight, lips curled back, fangs bared. Cooper knew enough not to get hit or grabbed. Vampires were stronger than mortals. Dropping the gun, he pulled the flashlight from his pocket, flicked it on, and aimed it at Quinn's face.

When the artificial sunlight hit Quinn's eyes, he stumbled and cried out, momentarily blinded. Cooper rushed forward and swung. His machete penetrated about halfway through Quinn's neck, and the man fell.

Dropping the flashlight, Cooper raised the blade with both hands and swung downward, this time taking the head off. By the light of the flashlight on the ground, Cooper could see blackish blood pouring out in the dirt, but he didn't hesitate. Leaving the flashlight where it lay, he grabbed up his gun and ran back into the cabin.

It took a few seconds for him to absorb what was happening. Somehow, Lee had dropped his gun, and it lay on the floor. James, the older man with the shaved head, had a hold of Lee's right arm and was slamming it into the wall, trying to make him drop the machete.

Nathan, with bullet wounds in his leg and head, was partially up and moving toward the gun on the floor. At the sight of Cooper, he hissed and scrambled faster, but Cooper rushed, shooting him in the face to stun him and then swinging downward. He missed and caught Nathan's jaw. Jerking the blade back up, he swung again. His aim was better, and he cut most of the way through Nathan's neck. One more hard swing finished the job.

Looking up, he saw Lee punching James in the face with his left fist, trying to throw him off. Lee's expression had taken on a wild quality that sometimes came over him during a fight. More than once, he'd become so lost in a battle that it could be hard to bring him back even when the fight was done.

Cooper had only two bullets left.

Raising his gun, he shot James twice in the back, causing the vampire an instant of pain. Lee shoved him off and then kicked him backwards. The instant James was an arm's length away, Lee swung, taking his head off in one motion.

The girl was still crouched in the corner, watching.

But as the body dropped and the head bounced once on the floor, she cried out. Snarling, Lee strode over and grabbed her wrist, jerking her up and drawing back his machete.

"Lee! No!" Cooper rushed forward, catching Lee's arm. "Look at her!" Somehow, he got Lee to stop. "Just look at her."

Maybe sixteen years old, she was small, barely over five feet tall, with light brown hair down past her shoulders. She was bone-thin, with wounds on her neck and wrists. Her expression was lost and terrified. Quickly, Cooper reached out and lifted one side of her upper lip. She had no fangs.

"Let go of her," he ordered.

Lee let go.

As soon as she was free, she stumbled over to James's headless body and sank slowly to the floor, letting out a sound like something from a wounded animal.

She began to choke and then looked up to Cooper with tears running down her face. "My... my... faaa...ther."

At first, he didn't understand, and then he asked, "That's your father?"

She was sobbing now. "They... chhhh... change him. They come through the d... door and they chhhh... change him. Burke brought us h... h... here." She leaned over her father's body, keening softly.

Cooper still didn't fully understand, as her speech patterns were difficult to follow, but vampires had turned her father, and she'd somehow ended up with him here—but no one had turned her.

"We need to get out of here," Lee said, still panting, but sounding like himself again. "Our part's done. The sheriff will need to start the cleanup."

Cooper blinked several times and then shook his head. "We can't leave her like this."

Lee started for the door. "The sheriff will take care of it."

"No." After setting down both of his weapons, Cooper crouched beside the girl and reached out, turning over one of her torn wrists.

She didn't fight him. "They drink," she whispered.

"If the sheriff comes out and picks her up," Cooper said to Lee, "he'll have her transported to the hospital in Roseburg. If they hear her like this, they'll put her in a psych ward."

Lee stopped in confusion. "Well, then, what do you want to do?"

"Take her with us. She needs time to calm down."

"Take her with us?" Lee repeated, sounding stunned. "Where?"

"Back to the motel." Cooper looked up. "Lee! She just watched you cut her father's head off. She needs some time." Without waiting for an answer, he reached for the girl, to help her stand. "Come with us," he said. "It's all right."

Like a child, she tried to obey, half stood and nearly collapsed. He caught her and picked her up. She weighed almost nothing, and her bones felt light in his arms.

"Bring my gun and blade," he said to Lee. "She's coming with us."

Carrying the girl, he walked out of the cabin, leaving all four headless bodies behind.

Cooper drove.

Since neither he nor Lee had eaten since lunch, he stopped at a drive-through long enough to pick up five burritos. In the back seat of the Jeep, the girl was awake, but she was quiet. Lee didn't say a word all the way back to the motel, but he sat with his jaw tight, and the silence was tense.

Pulling into a parking space near their room, Cooper said, "Don't get out yet. We need to call this in." He took out his cell phone and called Damon Tucker.

"Cooper?" The sheriff answered on the first ring.

"It's done," Cooper said, "but there were four of them, including your missing persons. They'd both been turned. Nathan Summers killed the last victim, and I think Quinn Moore killed the others. We had to put both men down." He let that sink in and then continued. "The bodies are in an abandoned cabin out on Sweetwater Road. If you look at the heads, you'll find fangs."

The sheriff was quiet for a moment, and Cooper was well aware of all the messy loose ends. The vampires were dead. The threat was resolved, and the town was safe. But Sheriff Tucker had four headless bodies to handle, and then he'd have to report to Nathan's family and Quinn's mother that their missing loved ones were dead.

"All right," the sheriff finally answered. "I'll drive out there now. I'll contact you tomorrow about payment."

Cooper hung up.

For him and Lee, this was the way of things. They handled the threat, and the fallout was left to whoever had hired them. They were not responsible for the aftermath.

Or they never had been.

Not until tonight.

From the rearview mirror, he glanced into the back seat. He didn't understand why he'd done this. And Lee sure as hell didn't understand why he'd done it. But nothing would have induced him to leave this girl behind on the floor of that cabin crouched beside her headless father.

In the back seat, she was sitting up now, but her head was down. Exhaling slowly, he got out of Jeep and opened the passenger door.

"It's okay," he said. "Come inside with us."

Again, she obeyed him, letting him help her out and following him to the motel room door. Lee came behind carrying their dinner and some of their gear. Cooper unlocked the door and stepped in to turn on the light.

Blinking, she peered inside, and her gaze stopped on the kitchen sink. Then she ran forward, surprising him with her speed, turning on the water, and using her hands to gulp in mouthfuls.

"Jesus," Lee said, stepping inside. It was the first thing he'd said since leaving the cabin, but even he appeared affected by the sight of her gulping water as if she'd not had any in days. After setting down his burdens, he closed the door and locked it.

Both men watched the girl.

This was the first clear look Cooper had in good light. She wore a long skirt and what once might have been a sleeveless blouse. Her clothes were filthy and in tatters. Her feet were bare.

She continued drinking water from the faucet for nearly a minute. Then she turned and looked at them, and now, she seemed aware enough to be afraid. Fear passed through her eyes.

"I'm Cooper," he said. "And this is Lee. We just want to help you."

Her gaze shifted between them, but she didn't respond.

Lee took a burrito from the bag and unwrapped it. Taking a few steps forward, he held it out. "You hungry?"

Her attention fixed on the food, but she drew away from him, moving down the counter. Though Cooper was beyond grateful that Lee was actively helping now, he wasn't sure what to do himself.

Putting one hand up in the air, Lee said, "It's all right." He set the food on the counter and moved away. As soon as he was halfway across the room, she darted forward, grabbed the burrito, and then dashed back again, crouching in the corner between the kitchen and the bathroom, eating in small, rapid bites.

Cooper could not help flashing back to a memory of himself wolfing down a tuna sandwich and then licking his fingers.

She finished the burrito in a matter of minutes. Cooper would have given her another one, but if she'd been starved, it was better to start slow. After eating, she appeared less frightened of them. She was filthy, and although the wounds on her neck and wrists weren't bleeding, they needed to be cleaned and bandaged. He was considering how to suggest this when she peered into the bathroom at the shower. Then she looked down at herself, at her wrists.

Pointing toward the bathroom door, she asked, "May... I... may I..."

With the few things she'd said, she'd stuttered and stammered, trying to get the words out. But this might be due to shock and stress.

"You want to go into the bathroom?" he asked. He had a feeling she'd been without running water for some time.

She nodded.

Glad that she seemed more in control of herself, he answered, "Of course. Go ahead."

Quickly, she vanished into the bathroom and closed the door.

With some space to breathe, he turned helplessly to Lee. "I know we don't do this, but she's been through something, and she needs time to calm down."

To his profound relief, Lee nodded. "You're right. I'm sorry I was..." He trailed off and added, "You were right that if we'd left her, they would have put her in a psych ward."

"Yes, I just couldn't—"

He broke off when the bathroom door cracked.

"Coo... Cooper," she said quietly from behind the door.

Hurrying forward, he said, "You need something?"

Cracking the door a little wider, she held her soiled, tattered clothes in one hand. He saw she was wrapped in a towel. "So dirty," she said.

"Hang on."

Going to his own bag, he rummaged around and pulled out a long flannel shirt and a T-shirt. He also drew out their first aid kit. It wasn't much, but at least it contained Neosporin, gauze, and tape. This was the best he could do. Hurrying back, he held them out. "Here."

"Tha... aa...thank you."

In spite of the stammering, she sounded better now, more coherent.

Once she'd taken the clothes and first aid kit from his hands and closed the bathroom door again, he heard the lock click. The sound of running water followed. He knew to some people, it might seem strange that she'd been through a horror show tonight, and after gulping water and eating some food, she was now tending to her wounds. But he could remember a time when he'd have done the exact same thing. It was more normal to care for yourself in desperate situations when you'd spent enough time having no one else to care for you.

Lee sat down to eat, and Cooper sat down at his computer. He needed something to do, something to focus on for a few moments, so he checked their website for messages. There were none.

"You need to eat something," Lee said.

"Yeah."

They sat at the table together without speaking, eating the burritos. They'd just finished when the water in the bathroom shut off, and a few moments later, the girl emerged. She looked as if she'd taken a shower, as her damp hair hung in waves. She wore Cooper's T-shirt with his flannel shirt buttoned over the top. The flannel hung to her knees. Her wrists were bandaged, and the wound on her neck appeared clean.

She stopped at the sight of his laptop computer on the motel room desk. Pointing, she asked, "Coo... Cooper, mmm... may I?"

This surprised him.

It must have surprised Lee as well, because he asked, "She wants to use the computer? Now?"

But Cooper stood up. Maybe she had a mother somewhere or someone she wanted to contact. The thought filled him with hope. If she had other family, they could deliver her someplace safe. "Yes. Of course. Do you want to use my email? We have phones too. Can we call someone for you?"

Without answering, she went over and sat down, but instead for calling up the email program, she clicked on his word processing program and began typing rapidly.

Standing behind her, he read as she typed, and his entire body went still.

"What?" Lee asked in alarm, looking at his face. "What is she typing?"

Cooper just stood there, reading.

My name is Beth McAdams. I have a severe speech impediment.

My father was a physics professor at the University of Washington. Seven years ago, he became disillusioned with academic departmental politics and resigned. He took us to live in a cabin in the Cascade Mountains. We were alone.

A month ago, two men broke through our door, and they changed my father. He would not let them change me. But when Burke left, he took us. He brought us to the cabin here in Oregon. I don't know where the other man went.

"What does it say?" Lee asked.

Cooper read the few passages aloud, and as he read, Lee stood and walked up behind them.

"Disillusioned?" he repeated.

Cooper understood what he meant. Perhaps they had both begun to think of the girl as somewhat simple due to her difficulty communicating. But she was not simple. She had trouble speaking verbally. That was all. Still, this was only a fraction of what was going through his mind. This girl, Beth, had been taken into the wilderness to live in a cabin with a misanthropic father for seven years, and then it appeared they had been discovered by a pair of vampires. After turning Beth's father, the pair had split up. Why? Burke had come here to southern Oregon and created two more vampires, for a nest of four. Again, why?

"Wait," Lee said. "That last vamp I killed was her father. He didn't look anything like a physics professor."

This struck Cooper as an odd statement. What did a physics professor look like? "That was seven years ago," he answered. "People change." Then he knelt down beside Beth. "How old are you?"

"Sev... sev... seventeen."

Her light brown hair was drying in soft curls around her face, and the waves flowed down past her shoulders. Her eyes were a shade of amber, and they almost glowed. Her skin was smooth and pale. Her nose was small above a heart-shaped mouth. It hit him then that she was shockingly pretty. For some reason, this worried him, but he wasn't sure why.

"Beth," Lee asked. "Where is your mother?"

"Dead." She said this without stammering.

"Do you have anyone else? An aunt or a family friend, someone we can take you to?"

She turned in the chair to face him. "No."

He frowned. "There must be someone."

She drew back a little at the urgency in his voice but shook her head. "No." She appeared exhausted.

"Lee," Cooper said. "Let's leave it for now. She needs rest."

It was getting late, and some sleep might do them all good.

For a moment, it seemed Lee was going to keep pressing, but he finally breathed out through his teeth. "All right. We'll figure this out tomorrow. Let's put her in the back bed. You can take the one near the door. I'll sleep on the couch."

"No... no." Beth stood, her face awash with concern. She touched Lee's arm. "You... sle... sleep in back bed. I sleep on the couch." Hurrying over, she sat on the couch and motioned around the room. "You and Coo... Cooper help me, find warm room with w... w... water. You bring food. C... C... Cooper gives me clean clothes. You are k... k... kind. I am smaller than you. I s... s... sleep on couch."

This was quite a speech from her, and Lee stood frozen, as if at a complete loss how to respond. Cooper had a feeling that she affected him greatly, and that he had no wish to be affected.

But Cooper moved quickly to get a blanket and pillow from a closet and then walked to the couch. "She is smaller," he said over his shoulder. If she wanted to sleep on the couch, he was going to let her do as she wished. Putting the pillow in place at one end, he said, "Lie down."

She obeyed him, and he covered her up.

"Let's all just get some sleep," he said.

In the middle of the night, Lee was awakened by the sound of screaming. Instantly, he sat up, ready to fight, confused for a few seconds as to where he was. The room was dark, but there was enough light coming in a window that he looked toward the sounds to see someone thrashing on the couch, and he remembered.

The girl.

Before he could react, Cooper hurried over to Beth, kneeling down, and catching her in his arms.

She fought him and cried out, "They're coming in the door!"

"Shhhhh," he said, holding her. "There's no one else here."

Lee clicked on a lamp.

Beth opened her eyes and sucked in air. She'd stopped screaming and was sobbing now. "Cooper?" She gripped his shirt with one hand and pressed her face against his shoulder. "They're coming in the door!"

To Lee's surprise, Cooper put one arm under her knees, the other around her back, picked her up, and stood.

She clung to him, crying. "They're coming in!" She didn't stammer or stutter in this half-sleep state.

"There's no one there," Cooper said, holding her off the ground like a child. Then he walked toward the bed where he'd been sleeping and put on her down with her head on a pillow. "Lie here." He ran his hand over her face. "It's all right. No one is coming in. You sleep here in the bed." He started to move away, toward the couch, but she grabbed his hand.

"No! Don't go. Y... y... you sleep here and w... watch the d... door." Her stammer was coming back. "You can see the d... door."

Lee wasn't sure what she meant.

But Cooper nodded and said, "Hang on."

Walking across the room, he took the blanket off the couch. Going back, he put her on the far side of the bed, away from the door, and covered her with the hotel comforter. Then he lay down on top of the comforter on the other side of the bed and covered himself with the blanket. "I can see the door from here. I'll watch it. You go back to sleep."

Calmer now, lying behind him, she closed her eyes.

Lee stared at the scene. Cooper was just going to sleep there in the same bed with her?

"You can turn off the lamp," Cooper said. "Everything is okay now."

Lee didn't know what to say, but as he turned off the lamp, he felt a knot in his stomach that somehow, everything was far from okay.

. . . . .

The next morning, Cooper woke up feeling something warm against his arm. He looked down to see Beth's face pressed against the outside of his shoulder, her hair draped over his arm. She was asleep. Carefully, so as not to disturb her, he moved away and then turned to get out of the bed.

Lee was already awake, fully dressed, down to his boots, sitting on his own bed and watching them.

"We need to talk," Lee whispered. "Outside."

Cooper had slept in his jeans and T-shirt. Without bothering to put on his boots, he followed Lee outside and closed the door behind them. They stood on the sidewalk in front of the motel. The sun was up, but he wasn't sure about the time.

"What's wrong?" he asked, genuinely confused.

Lee's entire body was tight. "The vamps are dead," he said. "So, we're done here. It's time you called the sheriff and have him pick up the girl. Or we can drop her off at the station."

"Drop her off?" Cooper felt his own body tense up. "We can't do that. She may not go to the psych ward now, but she's underage and doesn't know of any relatives. She'll end up in the system."

He kept seeing the same words on the computer screen from the night before.

He took us to live in a cabin in the Cascade Mountains. We were alone.

He knew what she'd suffered even before her father had been turned. He also knew what it was like to integrate back into the world. She would not survive in the foster care system.

Lee shook his head. "Well then, what do you want to do? Take her to a hospital?"

That would have the same result.

"No. She must have some family. With a father like hers, she may not know much. I didn't even know I had a grandmother until I was twelve."

"So, you want to stay here until you can track down a relative?"

"We should head home. There's no reason to stay here."

Lee's jaw twitched. "Home? You mean take her home with us? To Quinault?" He crossed his arms. "No! You and I made an agreement a long time ago. When the job's done, we're done. We don't deal with fallout, and we don't bring home strays."

"Strays? She's not a dog." Anger started rising. "Lee, she watched you cut her father's head off! I don't think our normal rules apply here, and I'm not leaving her to the system. We'll take her home, and I'll do the research. I'll track someone down."

Lee's eyes were hard and flat, and Cooper had never seen this side of him. Why would Lee be so opposed to bringing home a traumatized girl—one whom they had helped traumatize? He also knew there was more going on beneath their spoken words.

The truth was that the log house belonged to Cooper. Though Lee was a partner, the business belonged to Cooper. In the end, this decision was Cooper's. The two of them had never argued like this before, and he didn't like it.

But he was not leaving the girl behind.

"Let's pack up our gear," he said.

They were going home.

Chapter Four:

The Girl

While still at the motel in Mason Creek, Cooper spent some time on his phone with the sheriff arranging for final payment, and then he and Lee packed up the Jeep.

By the time they were finally ready to leave, and he was putting Beth into the back seat, he realized they couldn't possibly stop at a diner for breakfast as she was both barefoot and wearing only one of his T-shirts with a flannel shirt over the top. Her own clothes were so soiled and tattered that he left them behind in the kitchen trash can.

In the end, he opted for a McDonald's drive-through and bought them all Egg McMuffins with hash browns and orange juice, so they could eat in the Jeep. This time, she took the food from his hand, but again, she ate quickly.

It was nearly eleven o'clock in the morning by the time they pulled onto Interstate 5 to start the long drive home.

Since their argument out in front of the motel room, Lee had hardly said a word, and Cooper hated being at odds with him. Anger between them was new to them both, but he just couldn't figure out why Lee was so opposed to helping Beth.

They'd gone only a few miles when Lee said, "You going to keep her in the car all the way home?" He didn't sound angry now, just tense.

"We can't take her out dressed like that."

Not to mention the visible wounds on her neck.

"There's a Target in Eugene."

With everything going through his mind, Cooper hadn't thought about that—just stopping to buy her some clothes—and he was grateful that Lee was offering suggestions to help. This made him feel that at least in part, they were working as a team again.

So, when they reached Eugene, he pulled off and found the Target store.

"Beth, what size shoe do you wear?" he asked.

She had seemed a bit lost all morning, which was understandable given the circumstances. Though she'd followed his instructions, she hadn't spoken.

"S... s... six," she answered.

"Okay, you wait here with Lee. I won't be long."

Jogging into the store, he went straight to the junior's section. He had no idea what size clothing she might wear, so in the end, he bought some small drawstring pants, socks, a packet of underpants, and a pair of light gray canvas sneakers. She could wear his shirts for now. He also bought her a toothbrush and a hairbrush.

Walking back out to the Jeep, he motioned Lee to get out and then handed the clothes inside to Beth.

"Here. Put these on. We'll wait outside while you dress."

Upon taking the drawstring pants and shoes from the shopping bag, she looked up at him. "Oh, C...C...Cooper. Thank you."

For a second, he thought she was going to cry, and he closed the Jeep door quickly.

Then he stood outside with Lee with their backs turned. The parking lot was half-full, and the Oregon sun shone this morning, not offering much warmth but soft, hazy light.

Beside him, Lee breathed in and out a few times audibly and then said, "So, the plan is to bring her home and start trying to research any family?"

"Yes," Cooper answered, glad they were speaking of plans. "We have her father's name and a past place of employment in Seattle. There must be someone."

Lee nodded, seeming more resigned now. "Okay. I'm not trying to be a dick here, but this is a slippery slope. Trust me. I know. With what you and I... do for a living, we're going to make some widows and orphans. That's just part of the job, and we can't take responsibility."

Perhaps Lee was speaking of his military experience? Or was it something deeper? Though Lee was by far the closest friend Cooper had ever had, they rarely talked about their pasts. For them, their current life started the night they met. Cooper liked to think the past didn't matter.

But that wasn't true. Of course it wasn't true.

"When I was seven years old," he said, "my father took me and my mother to live in a shack in the woods out-side of Olympia, without much money or food. The nearest town was thirty miles away. He kept us there until I was twelve, and then he abandoned us. I don't think he even checked to see if we had enough gas to get down into town."

Lee turned to look at him. "What?"

Cooper didn't answer. He didn't know how, and thankfully, Beth tapped on the window.

"Done," she called.

Cooper walked around to the driver's side, and they got back on the road, but by then it was past noon. By the time they reached Portland, they hit early rush hour and ended up passing through the city at a slow crawl. The day was nearly over, and they hadn't even reached Washington State yet.

But the journey itself, inside the Jeep, was better than he'd expected. Beth seemed more comfortable now that she was fully dressed, and Lee seemed to have ac-cepted the situation with his usual good grace.

They didn't stop for a meal.

Still, it was eight o'clock by the time they pulled up to the log house in Quinault.

Lee opened the door to the back seat and motioned Beth out. To Cooper's surprise, she reached out and touched the back of Lee's hand for a few seconds. Then she climbed out of the Jeep, taking in the sight of the house and the trees all around.

"This is where we live," Cooper told her. "You'll stay here with us until we can find someone who knows you."

She blinked. "Who k... knows m... me?"

"Yes. Come on in."

"You two go on," Lee said. "I'll unpack the gear."

Cooper led Beth inside the living room. The floor was hardwood, with a few dusty area rugs. He couldn't help being embarrassed by the clutter all over the coffee table and end tables. There was a long couch, and an old easy chair, and a TV on a stand. Lee's half-empty coffee cup from Thursday morning was still sitting on Grandma Bea's bookshelves.

Beth didn't seem to notice the mess, and she looked through the open archway into the next room.

"Kitchen?" she asked clearly.

"Yes."

Walking through the arch, she looked around. Again, the kitchen was a mess—worse than the living room—but she went straight to the refrigerator and opened it, almost smiling at what she saw.

"T... t...trout."

Then he remembered he'd left three trout in there on Thursday. After only two days, they should be fine. Sometimes he or Lee would try to bake the trout they caught, but he was not up to attempting cooking tonight.

"I think there's some canned soup in the pantry. Maybe we should have that instead?"

Looking up from the fish, she seemed about to try to speak and then pointed to his jacket pocket. "Ph... phone?"

Puzzled by the turn of conversation, he drew out his phone. "You want to call someone?"

Hurrying over, she took the phone and scrolled through his apps to "Notes." Then she rapidly pecked out words and showed him the screen.

Please let me make dinner. I like to cook. Just give me about thirty minutes.

Her written voice was so different from her spoken voice. He was also becoming aware that her time isolated in the forest with her father may have quite different from his own experience. She knew how to use a computer and a cell phone.

"Beth, you just got here, and it's been a long day. You don't need to cook."

She typed again. *I would like to. Please.*

"Okay." He gave in. Maybe she needed something to do. "I'm going to go upstairs and see about a bedroom for you."

She nodded and turned back to looking through the fridge.

Heading back through the living room, he went upstairs, knowing there was only one room where they could put her. Lee's bedroom was the first door on the left. There were two other bedrooms, along with a bathroom at the end of the hall—with a tub but no shower. The shower was downstairs.

Both of the spare bedrooms were used for storage, but one of them contained a twin bed. Entering the room, he grimaced upon looking around. Lee stored spare truck parts in here as he didn't like leaving them in the carport.

There were a few boxes of old files on the bed.

Cooper moved things around to make a path, cleaned off the bed, and then found some sheets, a quilt, and a blanket in the hall closet so he could make up the bed. It wasn't much of a room for Beth, but at least she'd have somewhere private to sleep.

Glancing at his watch, he saw he'd been up here for nearly forty minutes, so he headed downstairs to see Lee coming in the front door. What had he been doing outside all this time?

Before he could ask, an aroma drifted to him, and he turned toward the kitchen.

"What is that?" Lee asked, sniffing the air.

They walked into the kitchen to find Beth dishing up three plates. There was a pan of biscuits on the counter. Cooper wondered where she'd found the ingredients to make biscuits, but there they were, looking light and fluffy and tan on top. There was a bowl of warm peas. He remembered they had a bag of peas in the freezer. She'd pan-fried the trout, and she was in the process of lifting a tail to remove all the bones in one motion. The other two were already done. She placed a boned trout on each plate, a biscuit, and a large scoop of peas. Then she found butter and a small honey bear for the kitchen table. She set the plates on the table with forks and folded paper towels for napkins.

It looked like... a meal.

Lee got two beers from the fridge and handed one to Cooper. Then he walked over to the table with some hesitation, as a woman in their kitchen was an alien sight. But Cooper knew Lee loved pan-fried trout and biscuits with honey.

"This looks good, Beth," Lee said finally. "Thank you."

She smiled.

The three of them sat down to eat.

.   .   .   .   .

Not long after dinner, Cooper showed Beth upstairs to her room. Once inside, she looked around, and for the first time, he saw a flicker of what appeared to be realization. Since last night, she'd been in shock, and he knew enough about human nature to know that what had happened to her father, what had happened to her life, had still not fully hit her.

It would.

"I know it's not much," he said to fill the silence. "But the bed has clean sheets, and if you're here longer than a few days, we'll figure something out."

"Will y... you check the c... c... closet and window?" she

asked, still looking around, frightened now. "They come in through the d... doors."

At that, realization flooded through him of what he'd agreed to take on. She was damaged, possibly broken, and he was in uncertain territory now. But he had a feeling he knew what she needed him to do, and he opened the closet, inspecting it while she watched, and then he went to the window.

"This window is locked tight," he said. "Come over and see." She came to him and he continued. "You're on the second floor. I sleep downstairs, and Lee will be in the next room. Nothing is getting in here. Understand?"

Hesitantly, she nodded, and he pulled back the covers on her bed.

"Come crawl in. You need some sleep." She obeyed him. He covered her up and walked to the doorway, clicking off the light. "I'm right downstairs."

After descending and emerging into the living room, he heard water running in the kitchen and followed the sound to find Lee doing the last of the dishes.

"Well, there is a sight to behold," Cooper said lightly. "You washing a dish."

"Shut up. She cooked. One of us can wash the dishes."

Cooper's moment of humor faded. He'd been wondering about something. "Lee, would you switch rooms with me tonight?"

"Why?"

"Because my room's all the way down here, and she's liable to wake up screaming again. I don't want you to have to deal with the nightmares."

Facing the sink, Lee kept his back turned. "It's no bother. I'll just sleep in my room. I had three sisters, and one of my older brothers was scared of his own shadow. I can handle a nightmare."

"You sure?"

"Yep."

.   .   .   .   .

Lying in a strange room that smelled vaguely of motor oil, Beth pulled the covers up around her neck.

She was afraid, but she was used to feeling afraid, as it was her normal state of mind.

For so long now, her life had felt like a series of things happening around her, things over which she had no control, starting with the day, when she was ten years old, that she'd walked into the bathroom in her family's large house in Seattle and found her mother dead on the floor.

Her father, James McAdams, was a strong man, both in body and spirit, and he expected strength from others. Beth's mother had been a fragile woman, both in body and spirit, and she'd not been able to live up to her husband's standards—or least this was how Beth viewed the situation later, once she was old enough to consider it.

As a child, she only knew that her mother often took pills that were meant to help her feel better, to help her be of more use to her husband. Beth's father approved of the pills. He approved of anything that would make his wife of more use. He never said this out loud, but Beth knew he approved because on occasion, she'd had the opportunity to touch the skin on one of his hands or arms, and she could feel what he felt inside.

She didn't do this often because he was cold inside.

Her mother, Helen, did not work outside the home. Her mother's job was to both attend and host dinner or cocktail parties to help James with his career. She was never comfortable in this role, and Beth remembered her mother often begging to be released from one social function or another.

"Please, James," she would say. "I'm not feeling well."

This always angered him, and an argument would follow—with him recounting his wife's many shortcomings. Beth wished he would be kinder and not say such things, as she often hugged her mother or held her hand and therefore knew how much her father's words hurt. But Beth herself would try to hide during these scenes, to make herself as small as possible. She did this at her mother's counsel.

"Beth, never challenge your father. Try to stay out of his way, and when you can't, do whatever he asks of you. He values only people he sees as useful."

Thankfully, James was not often home, as he worked late at the university to further his career. She knew he taught physics, but teaching seemed only a small part of what he did, and it was very important that he also published papers and collaborated with colleagues—and that he attended and hosted departmental parties.

When he was not home, the four-bedroom Tudor house in the Montlake area of Seattle was a comfortable place. Beth's mother was different when he wasn't there, bright and chatty. In the evenings, she and Beth would read books together or play cards, or sometimes when Helen had taken too many pills, they would lie in bed and just whisper secrets to each other.

Beth felt loved, and she did not feel alone.

When she was ten years old, her father found himself in competition with another man for a position called "Department Chair."

The arguments between Beth's parents grew uglier and more agitated than they had ever been. One Saturday afternoon, when Beth was not at school, she was in the kitchen getting a glass of milk when she heard her parents in the living room. Her mother was telling her father that she "was not up to" hosting a large dinner party scheduled for the following weekend.

Beth's father exploded.

"For God's sake, Helen," he shouted. "Do you understand how important this is? I'm out there killing myself for this position, and you do nothing! Nothing! I'm paying for a maid to clean the house because you're 'not up to it' and now you say you can't handle one dinner party? How lazy can you be? Have the Goddamned dinner catered if you need to, but get the house ready, order the wine, and buy a dress. Do you think you can manage to order centerpieces for the table?"

"Please, James," she whispered. "I can't have all those people here. I can't..."

"You'll be fine. Take a Xanax if you have to."

The argument went on for a while, and it ended, as it always did, with Beth's mother crying and promising to try. Her father stormed off to his den and closed the door. Her mother walked into the kitchen, still crying, and saw Beth.

She stopped. "Did you hear all that?"

Beth didn't answer.

Leaning on the counter as if needing support, her mother tried to smile. "Why don't you run down to the library annex? You can check out a copy of *Little Women* for us to read together later. Wouldn't that be fun?"

Relieved at the chance to leave, Beth nodded and hurried for the front door.

She took her time at the library annex and did not go home again for several hours. But upon arriving back at the house, she couldn't find her mother in the kitchen, living room, or formal dining room. She wasn't in her bedroom either. The door to her father's den was still closed.

Time passed.

Finally, Beth went into her mother's bedroom and knocked at the closed door of the private bathroom.

"Mother? Are you in there?"

When no one answered, she opened the door and saw her mother lying there with two empty bottles of pills on the floor beside her.

That was the last moment Beth ever did anything of her own accord.

Events moved swiftly from there... to the paramedics coming... to the small funeral... to her father shouting into the phone in his den. Something about Beth's mother's death caused her father to not become the new department chair.

As angry as he'd been before, his anger turned harder, more silent. Beth avoided even brushing the back of his hand with her own, as she didn't want to feel what he felt. She began having trouble speaking, terrified to say the wrong thing. She would try to be calm, to get the words to come out, but the more she tried, the more they seemed to stick, and they sometimes became jumbled inside of her head.

Two months later, her father came through the door in the early evening and really *looked* at Beth, as if he'd never seen her before.

"Pack a suitcase," he said. "We're leaving."

He drove them into the mountains. The journey took hours, and Beth felt trapped in the front seat of the car. Always before, any time her father had attempted to interact with her—to point out her shortcomings or faults—her mother had somehow interfered and distracted him. It had never occurred to Beth that her mother had been like a wall, protecting her.

Now that wall was gone.

She'd not even been allowed to mourn her mother, as her father was so angry about his wife taking (as he put it) a "coward's way out." Beth didn't know how to talk to her father. She had no idea what to say to him, and she feared the way he looked at her when she stuttered now.

In the mountains, he drove them up a long dirt road to a cabin surrounded by trees. When they stepped inside, Beth saw that though it was dusty, it was well-furnished with couches and low tables and seascapes on the walls of the living room.

"This has been in my family for years," her father said. "My father left it to me."

"How l... long will we st... stay?" Beth asked, speaking for the first time since leaving the house in Seattle.

"For good," he answered.

She didn't understand. "Wh... what a... about my sc... hool?"

He looked at her sharply. "I can teach you better than those fools at your school. And slow down when you speak! If you speak slower, you won't stammer. You'll never be of use to anyone if you can't speak clearly."

Although she had been lost in sorrow and loss at her mother's death, that was the first moment she felt fear. With her mother gone, Beth had now become his focus.

But he turned away from her and went back outside to begin unpacking their car. When she followed to help him, she saw that he'd brought numerous bags of groceries inside the trunk.

He also unloaded several boxes of books.

Over the next few days, she familiarized herself with their new home and found the place itself quite pleasing. It was smaller than their house in Seattle, but because of this it was easy to heat. The cabin had dependable electricity, two bedrooms, a large bathroom, a full kitchen, and running water from a well. It even boasted a stacked washer and dryer inside a closet off the kitchen.

Her father had bought his laptop computer, and he set this up at one end of the kitchen table.

They ate canned soup for dinner on the first two nights, and then on the third night, he asked her, "Beth, do you know how to cook anything?"

When he said this, it sounded like an honest question, as opposed to a judgment, but she knew if she spoke, she would stammer and annoy him. At her private school in Seattle, she had just begun learning to type. After glancing at his computer, she hurried over and sat down, typing.

I can make scrambled eggs.

Coming up behind her, he read the words and didn't seem angry at her sudden switch in method of communication.

"All right. Good. Maybe you could make us some eggs for dinner. See what else you can learn to cook. It is essential to be useful."

This time, she did reach out and touch his arm, reinforcing her prior understanding that his final sentence was the center of his moral code: the importance of being useful. In the weeks that followed, it became clear that his method of being useful was to see to her education.

One by one, he opened the textbooks and began lessons to teach her calculus, algebra and geometry.

Even at the age of ten, she gained a basic grasp of what he was saying. He'd brought books to teach her world history, philosophy, and literature. He discussed the mathematics of music, and he took her outside at night to point out the constellations.

They did not have internet service at the cabin, but before leaving Seattle, he'd downloaded a number of books, and she became accustomed to reading on his computer. He soon became more comfortable with her communications via writing (as he did not care for the sound of her stutter), and after a month, when he drove them into a town called Cle Elum to buy groceries, he stopped at an office supply store and bought her a tablet computer. With the tablet, she could carry it with her and much more easily communicate with him.

Occasionally, she did try to speak, but his face would darken at her struggles. "Slow down! If you would just calm down and slow down, you wouldn't stammer."

His anger only made her more anxious.

And he preferred her written voice. She knew this.

Years passed.

By the time she was fifteen, they were studying Socrates, Plato, Carl Jung, and Friedrich Nietzsche. With literature, her father was particular about what she read. She studied Chaucer and Moliere. He would allow her to read Shakespeare's tragedies and histories—but no comedies. If he was especially pleased with her, he'd allow her to read a Charles Dickens novel, which he viewed as little more than entertainment.

Each year, she became more skilled at cooking. She cooked all their meals, kept the cabin clean, and did their laundry. In the summers, they put in a vegetable garden, and she tended it. Nearly every day, her father impressed upon her the importance of being useful, and he often pointed out her shortcomings. Still, she knew he valued her.

He had not viewed her mother as useful and therefore had not valued her.

Beth feared what might happen should he stop valuing her. She needed him.

But he was not much company, and she felt alone. His only method of communication was to teach her something. Her only method of communication was to write a response to him on her tablet. They saw other people only when they drove down into Cle Elum for supplies, and Beth rarely spoke to anyone, even the checkers in the grocery store.

She did find some board games in a closet upstairs, and her father would play the ones he deemed non-frivolous, such as chess and backgammon. But sometimes they played Risk, which he considered a strategy game.

His hair began to thin, and one day, he went into the bathroom with a pair of shears and shaved his head. He said this would be less bother, and that he needed to focus all his attention upon her education.

By the time she was seventeen, her father was teaching her graduate-level calculus. He had her read Shakespeare's *Henry V* and write him a ten-page essay on the subversive subtext of the play. She sometimes wondered if life would ever change or if the two of them would live here like this forever.

Then one night, as she was just about to start making dinner, someone kicked in the front door of the cabin...

Lying in bed, in her room in Cooper's house, she closed her eyes and fought to hold off the memories. Too often, she relived that moment of their door being kicked up and the horror that followed.

With the blankets pulled up around her neck, she tried to breathe slowly, to make herself calm, to keep the memories away. Footsteps sounded out in the hallway, and she froze. The footsteps were steady and even —too heavy to be Cooper's—and she heard someone enter the bedroom next to hers.

It must be Lee.

He didn't like her, or at least he didn't like the idea of her being here. She'd touched the back of his hand earlier today and felt what he felt inside. Cooper was the one who wanted to help her. They didn't argue in front of her, but she was well aware of both their feelings. If she wasn't allowed to remain here, she had nowhere to go. She had to show Lee that she could be useful.

But now her challenge was to sleep. She needed to get some sleep, and yet she couldn't take her eyes off the window or the door. After lying awake for what seemed a long time, she quietly got up and lifted the blanket, the quilt, and her pillow. Leaving the bedroom, she stepped out into the hallway and saw that Lee had left his door half open. Peering inside, by moonlight coming in the window, she could see him asleep in his bed.

Silently, she crept in and made herself a bed on the floor directly beneath where he slept, using the folded quilt as a makeshift mattress. Then she covered herself with the blanket and laid her head on the pillow. He may not want her here in this house, but if anything came through the window or the door, he would kill it, just as he'd killed Burke.

Of this she was sure.

Finally, she was able to close her eyes and go to sleep.

. . . . .

From his bed, with one eye, Lee watched the girl come into his room and lie down on the floor. He didn't move.

Soon, her breathing grew even, and he could tell she was asleep.

He should have told her to go back to her room, as she was already becoming too dependent here. The sooner she learned to sleep in a room alone, the better. But he said nothing, and he did nothing.

Somehow, he knew she needed to sleep in here on the floor, with him up above. Something about her pulled at him. Last night, when she'd given her faltering speech about being grateful for all they had done for her and how she would sleep on the couch because he deserved to sleep in the bed, it had felt like she was reaching inside his chest.

This couldn't go on.

But he had to trust that it wouldn't. Tomorrow, Cooper would work his magic and do the research and find Beth some long-lost relative, and they would deliver her as soon as possible.

So, for now, if she needed to, she could sleep on his floor.

CHAPTER FIVE:

THE TRIAL RUN

The next morning, Cooper woke up wanting a better idea of Beth's past, of her life, as this would help him in his search for a relative or even a close family friend. By the time he emerged from his room, he could smell coffee coming from the kitchen, and he walked down the hall.

She was already cooking, and Lee was sitting at the table, drinking a cup.

"Good morning," Cooper said. "Sleep well?"

"Like a bear in winter," Lee answered.

Cooper hadn't heard any disturbances from upstairs in the night, and if Beth had been troubled by bad dreams, neither she nor Lee mentioned it.

Coming quickly to Cooper, she handed him a cup of coffee. Her hair hung in messy waves.

He took the cup but said, "Beth, you don't need to serve us coffee, and you don't need to make us breakfast."

Ignoring him, she went back to the stove and poached their last three eggs. He would need to go shopping for groceries today. She was also still wearing his T-shirt and the drawstring pants he'd bought yesterday, and she needed some more clothes. His "to do" list was growing.

After taking the pan of leftover biscuits from the oven where she'd been warming them, she made up three plates of biscuits with butter and poached eggs.

Cooper liked poached eggs but ate them only in restaurants, as he didn't know how to make them. Apparently, she was determined to cook. With a sigh, he sat down to eat. She placed a plate in front of Lee and then sat down as well.

After taking a few bites, Cooper asked her, "Beth, do you have any grandparents?"

This got Lee's attention, and he looked up from his breakfast.

But Beth shook her head. "No."

"Are they all dead?" Cooper asked, well aware this was an awkward question, but he had to know.

She thought on this for a moment, and then reached out for his phone sitting across the table. After typing for a moment, she handed it to him.

My father's parents both died in a car accident before I was born. My mother never mentioned her parents.

That wasn't promising.

"What about an aunt or uncle? Did either of your parents have a brother or sister?"

"No."

He was about to ask about family friends when he thought better of the question. If she'd lived alone with her father in a cabin in the Cascade Mountains for seven years, she probably wouldn't remember old family friends.

He could see she was becoming unsettled by his clear disappointment, so he said, "Don't worry. I was just looking for a place to get started. I'll get online today, and I'll make some phone calls."

They all finished breakfast, and by way of an answer, Beth got up and began clearing the table.

"You cooked," Cooper said. "Let me do that."

"No. P... please. Let m... me clean up."

He didn't know what to say.

Lee stood, as if wanting to be someplace else. "I'm going finish putting that carburetor into my truck."

· · · · ·

After getting her one of his clean T-shirts and showing her the downstairs bathroom—so she could take a shower—Cooper waited until he heard the water come on and then sat down at the kitchen table with his computer, using the privacy to get started.

The first thing he did was research James McAdams in the physics department at the University of Washington. Although James hadn't taught at the university in years, a bio did come up in a Google search, and Cooper found himself looking at a photo. James was younger in the picture, maybe late forties, with a full head of brown hair. He wasn't smiling.

He'd completed his doctorate at the California Institute of Technology and then moved to the Pacific Northwest, teaching for a few years at Washington State University in Pullman before being offered a tenure track position at the University of Washington in Seattle in 2003. That would have been around the time Beth was born. There was no mention of a wife or child in the bio.

There was nothing personal at all.

Cooper thought perhaps he would do best by trying to talk to someone, so he looked up the UW departmental directory and called the number for Computational Mathematical Sciences.

A woman answered. "Mathematical sciences. This is Maureen. How can I help you?"

Although he'd been prepared for this, for a second, he faltered, unsure how to begin. "Yes. I'm trying to track down any family members for Professor James McAdams. He taught physics for you until about seven years ago."

She answered, "I'm sorry, but we're not allowed to give out family information on past or present employees."

Her voice was business-like and brisk, and he feared she was about to hang up.

"I understand." Cooper was not fond of lying, but it came to him easily. "I'm sorry to say that Dr. McAdams was killed a few days ago. I'm with social services for

Thurston County. We have his daughter. She has a speech impediment, and we're attempting to track down anyone to whom she might be related. I'd like to keep her out of foster care if I can."

"Oh..." Maureen's voice altered completely, losing its brisk tone. "James is dead? You've got Beth?"

Whoever this woman might be, she'd worked for the university long enough to have known James and Beth.

"Yes. Can you do anything to help?"

"I can't. I didn't know his family except to meet them at a few functions. I'm just the office manager. But please hold. I think Dr. Hesford is in her office, and she worked with him most closely."

"Thank you."

This sounded more promising. Canned music came on the line.

Thirty seconds later, a quiet voice answered. "Hello? Maureen says you are from social services? She said James had died, and you have his daughter?"

"Yes. I'm trying to track down any family who might be able to help her."

The line was quiet for a few seconds. "Wouldn't she be sixteen or seventeen by now? Can't she tell you anything?"

"She's been through some trauma, and she has a speech impediment."

"Oh, I'm sorry. I didn't know."

"She has told me that her mother never spoke about parents. Could Beth have any grandparents on her mother's side?"

"On Helen's? I don't think so. Helen never talked about her family. I always had the feeling James was the only person she had, which made what happened even more tragic."

"What happened?"

"You don't know... Beth didn't...?" Another pause. "Helen committed suicide when Beth was about ten. Beth is the one who found her."

Cooper sat completely still.

"James was a difficult man," Dr. Hesford went on, "brilliant but lacking in human empathy. He functioned on an almost purely intellectual level. I wasn't the only one concerned about him sitting as a departmental chair, though he'd certainly earned it. But academic politics can be brutal, and Helen's suicide damaged his prospects. No one was surprised when he resigned. How did he die?"

"A car accident," Cooper lied. "Did he have any close friends, someone who might be willing to take Beth?"

"Friends? No, I don't believe James had any friends. He and I collaborated on a few papers, but as I said, he was a difficult person. I didn't know him well."

"Can you think of anyone else I might contact?"

"No. I'm so sorry I can't help, but to the best of my knowledge, James didn't have anyone in his life besides his immediate family. What will happen to Beth now?"

"I'll keep looking. Thank you for your time."

He hung up with the first moments of real doubt creeping in. He had believed he could find someone connected to Beth, but if Dr. Hesford was the closest thing James had to a friend, then talking to people was not going to help him here.

Cooper tried Ancestry.com and Genealogy.com next, searching both James and Helen. He found that Helen's maiden name had been Johanson, but she had no siblings, no father's name listed, and her mother was dead.

He found nothing further for James than what he already knew.

Down the hallway, the bathroom door opened and Beth emerged, dressed and towel-drying her hair.

Cooper closed his computer, a sinking feeling in his stomach, but he smiled at Beth. "I'm going to go grocery shopping. Do you want to come with me?"

She looked around the house. "Could I st...stay here?"

"Sure, if you'd prefer."

She looked back to him. "Could I m... make you a grocery list?"

"A list?"

Lee stayed out in the carport, putting a new carburetor into his truck. Mid-morning, he saw Cooper head off in the Jeep to go grocery shopping and knew his friend would be gone for some time. There was small, general store in Quinault, but for large runs, they went to the Safeway down in Aberdeen.

Throughout the afternoon, Lee glanced at the house a few times, knowing Beth was in there by herself and thinking he should at least check on her.

But he didn't.

This morning, when they'd both woken up, he'd pretended there was nothing unusual about her sleeping on his floor, and she had looked at him with gratitude. Something about her pulled at him. She pulled at his protective instincts, and he had no wish to be pulled at.

Instead, he let himself get lost in the engine of his old Ford pickup, and the hours passed. He didn't pay attention to the time until he heard the Jeep pull back in and noted it was after five o'clock. Cooper had been gone a long time.

Wiping his hands on a rag, Lee walked toward the Jeep to see the back seat loaded with bags.

"You buy the store out?" he asked.

Cooper climbed out a little wearily. "Just about. You should have seen the list Beth gave me. Then I ran to the Ross store to see if could find her some more clothes. But I don't know what size she wears, so I bought a few dresses, a sweater, and some pajamas."

While this all sounded sensible, the sheer amount of groceries in the back of the Jeep appeared... long term. Lee frowned. "What are we going to do with all this once she's gone? Neither one of us is much of a cook."

Turning away, Cooper said, "We'll figure it out. Here, give me a hand."

Together, they each carried armloads of groceries toward the house, but upon walking though the front door, Lee stopped. Cooper stopped beside him, wordless.

"What in...?" Lee asked.

The living room was clean, and not just tidied. It was *clean*. All the clutter was gone, and the area rugs had been vacuumed. The hardwood floor was polished. The furniture was dusted. The windows had been washed.

Looking through to the kitchen, Lee could see the dining room table and the counters had been cleaned. The place was immaculate.

"Did you tell her she could do this?" he asked tightly.

"No," Cooper answered carefully. "But she's probably just trying to help out, and it does look nice."

Still carrying two armloads of groceries, Lee whirled angrily. "We're not two of the seven dwarves, and she's not Snow White come to save us from ourselves! You can see what she's doing here, can't you? She's trying to make herself useful."

"Is that so bad?"

"No, it's not bad, but—."

He cut himself off as Beth came hurrying toward them from the kitchen. She looked so small in Cooper's flannel shirt.

"Did you g... get everything?" she asked, going to Cooper and looking into the bags.

"Yes. I think so."

Unwilling to continue the previous conversation in front of her, Lee walked into the kitchen to set down his burdens. For once, there was space on the counter. The entire kitchen was clean. It did look good, like a real home, and he liked it.

That's what pissed him off the most.

"I need to go put my tools away," he said. Then he walked out.

. . . . .

Cooper felt helpless as Beth whisked the bags from him and began putting groceries away. She nodded in approval as she drew one item after the next from the bags, keeping some items out that she apparently planned to use.

He could feel it was going to be cold tonight, even in April, so he left her to work, and he decided to build them a fire in the woodstove in the living room. He hadn't felt this conflicted in years, and he had no idea what he was going to tell Lee about his failed search for Beth's family.

Taking his time, he brought in wood, got some kindling lit in the stove and then crouched in front of it, feeding in split pieces until he had a full fire going. Then he stayed sitting there, watching the flames and thinking.

He wasn't sure how much time had passed when Lee walked back in the front door, still appearing tense.

But Lee only said, "A fire's a good idea. It's getting cold out."

"I bought more beer," Cooper said, closing the small door of the wood stove and avoiding any kind of real topic. "You want one?"

"Sure."

As soon as they walked toward the kitchen, an aroma wafted to Cooper, and he looked toward the oven to see Beth taking out a large pan of enchiladas. There was a pot of Spanish rice on top of the stove. Cooper paused at the sight. Lee's favorite dinner in the whole world was enchiladas and Spanish rice. How could she have guessed that?

As if forgetting his tension, Lee strode over and took a whiff. "Beth, this looks great." Then he looked back to Cooper. "You bought the stuff for enchiladas and Spanish rice?"

"I don't know. I just bought what she put on the list."

In truth, not everything on that list had made sense to him, and he wasn't used to buying produce, raw meat, and "ingredients." He and Lee tended to buy things that were ready-made.

Beth set the table quickly while Cooper took a few beers from the fridge.

"Beth," he asked, "do you want a glass of water or some of this lemonade?"

"The l... lemonade."

They sat down, and Cooper took a few bites. The

cheese was melted perfectly, and the enchiladas had just the right amount of spice. The rice was soft without being wet.

Lee was working his way through his plate almost without bothering to chew.

Beth had brought Cooper's phone to the table. Picking it up, she typed something and handed it to Lee. He stopped eating long enough to read what she'd written.

"The carburetor? It's going well. I should be able to take the truck for a test drive tomorrow."

Cooper smiled. "You actually going to have that thing running?"

"It's nearly always running. I'll just have it running better."

They ate dinner while talking easily about Lee's ancient truck—that was not running at least half the time. When the meal ended, Beth walked over to a side closet where Grandma Bea had stored the board games.

Pointing up, Beth said, "Lee?"

Walking to her, he looked up at the largest box. "Risk? I didn't even know we had this. Cooper, have we ever opened this closet?"

"Can we p... play?" Beth asked.

"You want to?" Lee appeared beyond pleased. "You sure? I played about a million games of this in the army, when we had nothing else to do. And I tend to take over Asia and Russia as soon as possible."

She smiled at him. "I t... take over E... Europe."

"Well, you give that a try and see what happens," he said, reaching up and taking out the box.

He looked cheerful, almost happy. Cooper had had no idea that Lee enjoyed playing Risk, but somehow, Beth had known exactly what to do.

"I'll wash the dishes while you two set up the game," Cooper said.

Twenty minutes later, they were around the table rolling dice. True to her word, Beth focused on Europe, while Cooper focused on North America, South America, and Canada. Lee rolled well and somehow managed to take over all of Asia and Russia. Then he began attacking in earnest.

They played until ten-thirty, but it was clear for about the last hour that Lee was going to win.

He did.

Beth smiled as she started to clean up the pieces. "That was f... fun."

"It was," Lee agreed.

Then she yawned, and Cooper remembered she'd been scrubbing floors and washing windows all day. He said, "You should go on up to bed. I can pick up the game."

But a flash of anxiety passed through her eyes as she glanced toward the stairs, and he remembered the routine from last night. "Do you want me to come up and check the windows and closet?"

Dropping her gaze, as if embarrassed, she nodded.

"What's this?" Lee asked.

"Oh, she just likes me to check the room and make sure it's safe," Cooper answered, not sure what else to say.

"I can do that," Lee said. "Come on, Beth. You look done in."

He headed for the stairs, and she followed him. Once they were out of sight, Cooper sighed as he looked down at the now scattered game. Tomorrow, he could pretend to go on with his research in finding a relative or a family friend to take Beth, but he knew he wouldn't find one.

He'd known that almost as soon as he'd finished speaking with Dr. Hesford at the university.

What was he going to do?

Slowly, he began picking up plastic army figures and putting them back in the box. The night had been enjoyable. He couldn't remember the last time he'd played a board game, maybe not since before Grandma Bea died. But he could not stop worrying about what would happen over the next few days. He was nearly finished putting away the game when Lee came back down the stairs and into the kitchen. Cooper's face must have betrayed him because Lee's expression shifted to alarm.

"What's wrong? What's happened?"

"Nothing has happened... it just..."

"Just what?"

Cooper decided he may as well get this out.

"Beth doesn't have any family. No grandparents. No aunts or uncles. There are no family friends. Her father was some kind of loner, maybe worse than a loner. Her mother committed suicide when Beth was ten."

"Suicide? Jesus." Lee ran a hand over his face. "And you're sure there's no one else? You've only been looking for a day."

"There's no one else. She's alone." Cooper paused and took a breath. "I know I pushed you into letting me bring her here. I thought I could find someone for her. But this place is just as much your home as mine. If you don't want her here, I'll take care of it. This is on me."

Lee hesitated. "What would you do?"

Misery hit him. "I'd drive her to Olympia and turn her over to social services." He knew his voice sounded as pained as he felt, but he couldn't help it.

"No," Lee said. "I don't want that. But I still believe we *can't* start taking responsibility for fallout."

Cooper straightened. "I know we can't. I swear I won't do this again, but with Beth... could we just let her stay here for now? Could we do this on a trial basis?"

Lee's expression was unreadable, but he nodded. "All right. A trial basis."

.   .   .   .   .

The following few days proved busy.

Now that the decision had been made, there was a great deal to be done. And upon contemplation, there were some decisions to be made. Cooper thought back to when his mother first brought him to Aberdeen.

She'd registered him with the public school system, and then he'd taken a series of placement tests. Quinault boasted a small high school, and Cooper wanted to keep Beth close to home, so he planned to register her there and get the ball rolling. She would need a high school degree in order to attend college.

But then he thought about her mental state and her speech impediment and wondered if online courses might not be a better option at first. How much power would he have over the situation? And then this made him wonder about how he was going to somehow play the role of legal guardian. Due to his heritage, he couldn't try to pass her off as a younger sister or even a niece, and for some reason, he didn't want to pass her off as Lee's sister. He wanted to be the one viewed as her guardian.

For once, he was thankful that no one had called to hire them for a job, as this gave him some time to think and plan.

In the end, they decided they would say Beth was Cooper's cousin—on his mother's side. They created a story that Cooper's aunt from Seattle had passed away, and Beth had come to live with them. She had no school records because she had been home-schooled. It wasn't much of a story, and it was paper thin, as Cooper's mother was an only child.

But it was the best they could do.

He started the paperwork with the high school, and in early May, Beth took her placement tests. Three days later, the vice principal emailed Cooper asking him to come in for a conference.

To Cooper's consternation, Lee insisted on attending as well. "I'm half of this now," he said. "I want to hear what these folks at the school have to say."

The following morning, the three of them climbed into the Jeep and Cooper drove them to the small high school. Beth was clearly nervous, even though she'd been here before to take her tests, and she kept close to Cooper. Her neck was nearly healed, with just a few red marks visible. Her wrists were healing more slowly, but she wore a yellow cotton dress he'd bought her with a long-sleeved, light blue cardigan sweater over the top, so her wrists were covered.

In the main office, they waited in plastic chairs until a slender woman emerged from a back office to greet them. She appeared surprised at the sight of Cooper and Lee with Beth.

"Good morning," she said. "I'm Vice Principal Sanders, Juliet Sanders."

But Cooper was equally surprised. She looked nothing like what he envisioned for a vice principal. For one, she was maybe thirty years old, and she was lovely, with long hair so dark brown it was almost black. Her eyes were just as dark, and her skin was a healthy tan shade that did not look artificial and could not have come from the sun at this time of year. She wore a white silk blouse over an olive-green skirt that came to her ankles. Small silver earrings in the shapes of feathers hung from her earlobes.

"I'm Cooper Reyes," he began. "Beth's cousin. This is my business partner, Lee Nevada. He'll be helping to look out for Beth, so he wanted to be here today."

Recovering quickly, she smiled at Beth. "It's so good to see you again, but I didn't expect you today. Would you mind waiting out here while I speak with your cousin?"

While Beth appeared anxious at the prospect of sitting out here alone, she also seemed to understand how important this was. "No. I d... don't m... mind."

Her stammer had been worse this morning, and Cooper noticed it became more pronounced when she was under stress. As he and Lee rose to follow Vice Principal Sanders, Lee raised one eyebrow at Cooper.

Could someone so young even *be* a vice principal?

Inside her office, Ms. Sanders closed the door. "Thank you for coming in. Please sit down."

Cooper felt like he'd been called in for some punishable infraction.

Sitting down behind her desk, she moved her gaze between them. "From what I've been told, Beth's mother passed away, and she's come to live with you, with the two of you?"

"Yes, ma'am," Lee answered.

For once, Cooper wished he would drop the semi-sarcastic charm.

"And there are no other possible family members?" she asked.

"No," Cooper answered. "My mother lives down in Aberdeen, but I thought Beth might do better in a smaller school. At first, she might even do better with online courses."

This seemed the right thing to say, as Ms. Sanders's tense posture eased slightly. "So, you realize you have some challenges here?"

"Challenges?"

She drew a folder from one side of her desk and opened it. "Beth's test scores are astonishing. She's in the 98th percentile in math, and the 97th in verbal."

"Compared to the other students here?" Cooper asked.

"No, at a state level. Principal Spencer and I are discussing how best to place her now. But while her academic scores are high, she will need speech therapy, and she suffers from severe social anxiety."

This set Cooper on edge, as he remembered hearing such things about himself when he was young—that he was somehow socially deficient. But he held his tongue. He couldn't do or say anything that might cause Ms. Sanders to look deeper into Beth's situation. A few phone calls could reveal that she was in no way related to him.

"I'd be glad to help set up speech therapy and pay for it," he said carefully.

"Can you tell me anything about her past that may help? How long has she had the speech impediment? What sort of home schooling was she receiving? Were there any domestic issues that could account for her lack of socialization?"

"I'm sorry, but I don't know much," Cooper answered. "My mother and her sister weren't close. When I learned that my aunt had passed away and that Beth was alone, I was afraid she might go into the foster care system, and she's not cut out for foster care. I had to do something."

This last part was true, and he could see it had an effect, but Ms. Sanders still appeared uncertain. And who could blame her? The real problem here was Beth's age. If she'd been nine or ten, this all might seem more normal. If she'd been eighteen, she'd be of legal age, and there would be no issue. But two men in their late twenties taking responsibility for a pretty seventeen-year-old girl?

Had he been on Ms. Sanders's side of the desk, *he* would certainly have concerns.

"I know this is an unusual situation," Lee put in, leaning forward in his chair. "But you should ask Beth what she wants. She'll tell you she feels safest with us. We've got a house and we earn a decent living. Coop and I can look out for her until she comes of age. We'll get her into speech therapy. We'll do anything you say, but he's right, and she doesn't belong in the foster system."

"I'm not here to judge you," she answered levelly, looking him in the eye. "I think what you've done is unselfish. Most people would see her as an inconvenience. I just wish I knew more. I could help her better if I knew more."

In that regard, Cooper wasn't going to say more than he already had. They couldn't very well tell her truth, that Beth had been living in an isolated cabin with her brilliant but cold physics professor father until he'd been turned into a vampire and Lee had cut his head off.

"I do think we should start with online courses if possible," Cooper said. "I don't think she could handle a normal classroom just yet, and you said she's already ahead of the curve in academics."

Ms. Sanders nodded. "I agree. The school year is nearly over now. She can start with some online courses this summer, we'll get her into speech therapy, and we can reassess in August. Does that sound all right?"

"Yes." Cooper breathed in relief. This conference felt like it was over, so he stood. "Thank you."

Lee followed him out of the office, but just outside the door, Cooper stopped at the sight of Beth, still in her chair, waiting for them.

They had her enrolled in school, and the administration viewed him as her guardian.

"Are we really doing this?" he asked softly.

Lee nodded. "Looks like."

CHAPTER SIX:

THE EMPATH

Over the following week, some of Cooper's worry eased as Beth became more and more a part of their daily lives. Lee had always wanted to put in a vegetable garden. For some reason, he liked the idea of growing their own tomatoes, potatoes, onions, and sugar snap peas. But neither he nor Cooper knew a thing about gardening. Although Lee never mentioned this to Beth, one morning, she brought them to an open area out back of the house and told them she knew how to plant and tend vegetables. That afternoon, they all drove down to Aberdeen together so that Lee could rent a rototiller and Beth could buy starters and seeds.

They prepped the soil and planted a garden.

Lee was pleased and said he couldn't wait for home grown tomatoes.

She cleaned and cooked and did the laundry, even when they told her not to. In the evenings, they played board games or watched movies from the DVD collection. It appeared she hadn't seen almost any movies, so it was enjoyable to introduce her to films they both liked—although Lee's tastes tended to lean toward war stories and Cooper preferred westerns or science fiction. She liked all three.

She was the perfect housemate.

Only two things troubled Cooper.

First, one morning when he woke up early, he went upstairs to see if Beth or Lee wanted him to get the coffee started, and he was alarmed to find her room empty. Over the past few days, they had been divesting it of engine parts and working on turning it into more of a "room" for her, but the bed had been stripped down to the sheets and she was not there.

He hurried to tell Lee and then paused in the door-way. Lee was asleep in his bed, and Beth was asleep on the floor, directly beneath him, on a makeshift bed of her quilt and blanket. Had she had a bad dream or maybe just a bad night?

Later in the day, he caught Lee alone and asked him.

"No," Lee answered. "She does that every night. She waits until she thinks I'm asleep, and then she comes in. I don't think she can sleep in a room alone yet."

She was too frightened to sleep alone in a room when she knew Lee was right next door? Lee did not seem bothered by this, but it worried Cooper. He'd thought she was improving... but maybe not.

The other thing that troubled him was her infallible ability to know exactly what they wanted to eat or how they might wish to pass the time. Three days after their meeting with the vice principal, they were home, and Beth was making lunch. Cooper walked to the counter to help her carry plates to the table.

She pointed to the nearest plate and said, "That o... one is yours. The other is for L... Lee."

As she was making turkey sandwiches with sliced apples on the side, he didn't see how it mattered.

But she picked up his phone, typed in a few sentences, and handed it to him.

Lee doesn't like peel on his apples, and you do. You don't like mustard on your sandwiches, but he does.

This was true, but Cooper had never told her he preferred apples with the peel left on—or that he didn't like mustard.

"Did Lee tell you that?" he asked.

She didn't respond and continued serving their lunch.

Four days later, in the afternoon, as he was splitting wood, an unbidden memory came to him, of Grandma

Bea's chocolate cake. He'd never much been one for sweets, but she made a dark chocolate cake that was almost bitter. He loved it and would eat half a cake if she'd let him. What would make him think of this? Maybe having Beth around was stirring up memories of how his grandmother always cooked for him.

Beth came out of the house to bring him a glass of lemonade, and when he reached for it, she touched his hand.

Then she went back inside, and he continued splitting and stacking the wood. When he finished, he took a walk down by the creek. He didn't bring his pole and just wanted to walk. He'd been thinking about the coming evening and thought it might be fun to show Beth *Star Wars*, as she'd never seen it.

By the time he got back to the house, it was early evening, and Beth was finishing making dinner: fried chicken, mashed potatoes, gravy, and corn on the cob. This was Lee's second-favorite dinner—after enchiladas and Spanish rice.

But there was a two-layer dark chocolate cake sitting on the counter.

"Did you make that?" Cooper asked her.

She nodded.

Halfway through dinner, she looked to him and said, "I t...thought we might watch Sta... ar Wars tonight."

"That sounds good," Lee said, taking a bite of fried chicken. "I haven't seen that in years. You've really never seen it?"

"No."

Cooper stared at her.

He was quiet for the rest of the evening. They watched *Star Wars* while eating chocolate cake, and Lee thoroughly enjoyed himself—as *Star Wars* was basically a war film set in space.

But when it was time for Beth to head for bed, Cooper said to her, "I'll check your room tonight. Come with me."

She glanced at him askance, as if his tone made her nervous, but she followed him up the stairs. Once inside the room, he motioned to the bed with one hand. "Sit down for a minute."

Cautiously she sat, and he looked around. He'd brought in a small antique desk and chair from the attic a few days ago, and he fetched the chair and positioned it so he could sit facing her. Her expression shifted to anxiety, and the last thing he wanted to do was frighten her, but they needed to talk. He had his phone in one hand.

Uncertain how to begin, he said, "Have I told you any-thing about my mother?" He knew he hadn't, but this seemed a good place to start.

She relaxed slightly. "Your m... mother?"

"She lives just down in Aberdeen, and she works as a psychic. Do you know what that means? She tries to help people make choices and decisions by pretending to know more than they do."

Beth watched him carefully.

"With my mother," he went on, "she can summon and channel spirits if she uses spellcraft, but most of the time, she just plays the psychic. She's not psychic. She's just very skilled at listening and then knowing what her clients need to hear, but when I was younger, your age, I met a few other people in the business, and two of them... two of them struck me as real, that they could pick up actual thoughts."

She dropped her eyes to the floor.

"Talk to me," he said. "You can tell me anything. How did you know that Lee loves enchiladas, loves to play Risk, likes his apples peeled, and that he's always wanted a vegetable garden?"

"I touched his h... hand," she whispered.

"What does that mean?" He held out his phone.

She took it and began typing words. Moving over to her, he sat down beside her to read.

I need to touch someone's skin, but if I do, I can feel what they feel and know what they know.

"You need direct contact? So, today, when you handed me that lemonade, you knew I was thinking about chocolate cake and *Star Wars*?"

"Yes."

Though he wasn't surprised, as he'd suspected something like this, he was no less troubled. He wasn't sure how Lee would feel about this. "Do you just pick up surface thoughts and feelings?"

She typed.

Unless I go deeper.

"What does that mean?" he asked.

Looking up at him, she slowly reached out with her free hand and lightly grasped his forearm. Her hand was so small. Then she closed her eyes. "Why did y... you bring me home?"

Instantly, his thoughts shifted to her telling them about her father taking her to a cabin in the mountains, then to his own childhood, to his father, to his mother, to how they'd lived, to feelings of isolation and loneliness and being unloved.

With a gasp, Beth let go of his arm as if he were on fire, and she took in a sharp breath. "Your faaa...ather, always with a gun. Hunting. And your mother! Cooper, I am so sorry."

She spoke the last sentence clearly, but he drew back. "You saw all that? In my head?"

"Y... you look at m... me and see yourself."

He fell silent. Yes, that was the truth, at least in part.

"Listen to me," he said finally. "You need to stop reading me and Lee and then spending your days doing things to make us happy. We both like having you here, and you don't have to try so hard. Do you understand?"

Carefully, she nodded, but he could see she didn't believe him. This might take some time.

Turning back to his phone, she typed.

Are you angry?

"That you can pick up on our feelings? No. Of course not." He paused. "But maybe we shouldn't tell Lee. At least not yet."

. . . . .

The next morning, just after breakfast, they were all still in the kitchen when the business cell rang.

"Permanent Solutions Unnatural," Cooper answered. "How can I help you?"

A breathy male voice spoke. "Yes, I'm the manager for the Columbia Gorge Hotel in Oregon. I was just read- ing through your website and..." He trailed off. "I'm not quite sure what to say."

Cooper carried the phone into the living room and sat on the couch. "It sounds like you need help with something you can't explain, and that's what we do. It's normal for clients to have trouble telling us what's happening." He paused. "My name is Cooper Reyes."

"Benjamin Jackson," the man answered, taking an- other breath. "I can hardly believe I even phoned you, but we're having some issues, and we're losing busi- ness. Our bookings for June are dropping by the day."

"What are the issues?"

"I know this will sound crazy, but guests are reporting being... possessed for short periods of time."

"Possessed?"

"Yes, they claim a spirit or presence of some kind is taking over their bodies. They claim being able to push it out, but the experience is traumatizing. I thought the first guest complaint was from someone who either wanted attention or was trying to get out of paying their bill, but then another guest complained, and an- other, all telling the same story. And now people are speaking out in public. They are writing negative re- views on Yelp! I don't know what to do. Have you dealt with anything like this before?"

Actually, they hadn't, but that didn't mean they couldn't solve it.

"We deal with a variety of issues. But my partner and I would need to come out and assess the situation."

"Yes. Good," Benjamin said, sounding relieved. "Please come. I need *someone* to handle this, and I certainly can't call the police."

"Our fee is twenty-five hundred a day plus expenses, but we can leave today and reach you by early evening."

"Just get here as soon as you can." The man sounded frazzled again but added, "Thank you."

Cooper hung up and walked back into the kitchen where Beth and Lee watched him expectantly. The kitchen still smelled of bacon, and Beth held a half-empty coffee pot in her hand.

"A job?" Lee asked.

"Yeah, in Oregon, at the Columbia Gorge Hotel."

Lee raised an eyebrow. "That fancy place on the river? Do we get to stay there?"

"Probably. I think we'll need to."

"What are we hunting?"

"A ghost... I think." Cooper quickly related what the manager had told him about guests reporting temporary possessions. "But he didn't mention any deaths or people suffering from hypothermia or frost bite, so I'm not exactly sure what we're walking into."

"We're rarely sure about anything. But I'll pack us up for a ghost hunt."

Beth set the coffee pot in the sink. "What should I p... pack?"

Lee turned toward her. "Pack? Nothing. You're not going. This could be dangerous. You need to stay here."

Her eyes widened in a mix of surprise and fear. "Here? A... a... alone?"

And in the moment, the reality of what they'd taken on hit Cooper in the face. They traveled for work, and their job was high risk, and she was not capable of remaining at the house alone for days and nights at a time.

But they couldn't take her on a ghost hunt.

"Beth, you know what we do for living," he said. "You need to stay home."

She rushed to him, shaking her head. "No... no."

He didn't know what to do or say, and Lee appeared stunned by this turn of her behavior—as if maybe he'd not thought this through either.

Quickly, Beth took the phone from Cooper's hand, and she began typing. He looked down.

Don't leave me here. I can help you.

"How?"

You will be questioning people. I can tell you who is lying, who is hiding something, and who is telling the truth.

He lifted his gaze to her face and studied her intense expression. That had not occurred to him. She could be of help, but he couldn't tell this to Lee. And how could they bring her into a ghost hunt? What if whatever they were hunting went after her?

I can't stay here alone. Please. Something will come through the door.

Her eyes were wild, pleading, and he suddenly knew they couldn't leave her.

Turning to Lee, he said, "We'll figure something out to keep her safe once we get there, but I don't think we can leave her here."

Lee's expression turned incredulous, but then he looked at Beth and didn't argue.

·　　·　　·　　·　　·

For Beth, the road trip to Oregon proved more enjoyable than she'd expected. At first, she'd just been relieved that Cooper and Lee weren't going to leave her alone at the house for days. How could she have made it through the nights?

Once they were in the Jeep, though, and she was in the back seat, sitting beside a pile of gear, she started wondering about the end of the line, where it sounded like they would be staying in an upscale hotel filled with strangers. Would she be expected to speak with these strangers herself? She couldn't do that.

But when they reached Aberdeen, Cooper took her to the Target store and told her to buy any clothing she liked. She was stunned. Her father had never allowed her to choose her own clothes. Still, she didn't hesitate long and quickly picked out jeans, white T-shirts, and an olive- green jacket. Cooper paid for them, and then he took her to the electronics department and bought her a cell phone with a rose-colored case. She could hardly believe it. She never been allowed her own phone.

They got back in the Jeep and back on the road.

Life with Cooper and Lee was so different from life with her father. Her speech impediment never made them angry, and they were so easy to please. They never found fault with her or lectured her on her shortcomings. Lee never made her feel like a coward for needing to sleep in his room.

Neither of them had read Moliere, Voltaire, or Dostoyevsky, but that hardly mattered. They looked out for her. And now they were they taking her on a road trip—on a job. Though she feared the prospect of interacting with strangers, she wanted to do everything possible to help. She'd need to watch them, to see how they began to solve this mystery of reports of ghost possessions, but she would look for ways to help. She wasn't afraid of the prospect of a ghost, as Lee had once related the worst thing a ghost could do was freeze a person to death, which sounded unpleasant but not terrifying. Ghosts were not like vampires who broke through doors, then tortured, maimed, drank blood, and sometimes changed people into monsters. She wanted to help Cooper and Lee with this ghost investigation. She owed them both a great deal for their kindness.

Cooper drove seventy miles an hour down Interstate 5 toward Portland. Then they would turn east down the wide Columbia River.

"You ever driven down the Columbia River Gorge?" Lee asked her.

"No." She'd never been much of anywhere.

He smiled. "It's beautiful. You just wait."

She smiled back. He cared that she was having a nice time.

For that alone, she'd have died for him.

CHAPTER SEVEN:

THE HOTEL

J udas Priest," Lee said as they pulled up to the Columbia Gorge Hotel.

Cooper couldn't disagree. This was not their kind of
place—which was usually a Motel 6. He knew this was a
historic hotel, built sometime in the early 1920s. They'd
driven past it several times while heading to jobs, but
they'd never been this close. It was constructed in the
mission style with a tan stucco exterior, a red-tiled
roof, and forest green trim. The hotel was surrounded
by carefully manicured gardens and situated near the
edge of the gorge with a view of the wide river below.

After parking, Cooper said, "Let's just leave everything
in the Jeep for now."

The manager, Benjamin Jackson, hadn't even officially
hired them yet.

All three of them climbed out, and Cooper led the
way to the main entrance and into the hotel. Before
leaving home, he'd prepared a contract and carried it
inside a manila folder. A middle-aged woman with a
pixie haircut stood behind the front desk.

She smiled. "Checking in?"

"The manager, Mr. Jackson, called us this morning.
We're here to assist him." He kept his wording deliber-
ately vague, but he didn't have to say anything more, as
a man came striding out of a back office.

"It's all right, Louise," he said, coming to the desk. "I'll
speak with them."

He looked to be late thirties with thinning hair and a goatee. He wore slacks, a white dress shirt and a dark blue blazer. His eyes moved from Cooper to Lee to Beth, pausing on Beth with a slight frown.

Quickly, Cooper stepped forward and shook the man's hand over the top of the desk. "I'm Cooper Reyes. We spoke on the phone. This is my partner, Lee Nevada, and our assistant, Beth McAdams."

With a nod, Benjamin said, "Yes. Come into my office."

All three of them walked around the side of the main desk and followed him. Cooper wasn't sure about bringing Beth into the interview but didn't know what else to do. He didn't want to just leave her sitting out here alone.

The back office was roomy but neat, sporting a dark wood desk with a leather upholstered chair behind it. An open laptop computer sat atop the desk. Large windows overlooked the patio. Cooper thought the hotel would not be a bad place to work for a person who could handle being tied to the same location all day—without the option of going home.

While walking toward his desk, Benjamin motioned toward the west corner with one hand. "Would one of you mind?"

Glancing over, Cooper saw four metal chairs stacked one on top of the other. Lee fetched three of them and set them up facing the desk. As the three of them sat, with Cooper in the middle, Benjamin settled awkwardly in his leather chair, appearing flustered to the point of embarrassment.

"I'm not even sure what to say," he began.

"That's not unusual," Cooper answered. "Nearly everyone who needs to hire us says that. But you read the testimonials on our website?"

"I did. Are those legit?"

Cooper never bristled when asked this question—and he was asked it quite often. "Yes. And you believe they are, or you wouldn't have called me."

Lee rarely spoke during an initial interview, and Beth sat quietly with her hands folded in her lap.

Benjamin sighed and leaned back. "Well, I have to do something. In addition to all the canceled reservations, last week one of my best maids claimed she'd been possessed... and she quit. After that, rumors spread like wildfire, and two of the restaurant's bus boys and one of our cooks quit. If this continues, we'll have no guests and no staff."

Cooper took this in. "Have there been any recent deaths?"

After an instant's pause, Benjamin shook his head. "No."

"What makes these people think they have been possessed?"

"How should I know! Isn't that your job? They report that *something* came inside them and took over their bodies and that it was terrifying. That's all I know."

"So, you haven't actually talked to anyone who's gone through this?" Cooper asked.

The question appeared to surprise Benjamin. "Talk to them? No. Why would I?" His expression hardened. "Is that what you plan to do? Talk to people? Because I'd rather not have that. I'd rather that none of our guests even know why you're here. I just want this handled as quickly and quietly as possible."

Cooper was trying hard not to dislike the man. Most people who contacted them genuinely wanted help. Even when expressing anger, the anger was covering distress or fear. But occasionally, they met someone like Benjamin who treated them like exterminators come to handle an ant infestation. Cooper had plenty of money in the savings account at present. He didn't need to take this job.

"We wouldn't go around advertising why we're here, but we would need a free hand if you want this figured out." He began to stand. "It's possible you'll need to hire someone who can offer complete discretion."

At this, Benjamin's features shifted to alarm. "What? No... please sit down. You must understand my position? The owners are furious, and they are blaming me."

Again. This was all about him.

But slowly, Cooper sat back down. "If we take the job, we'll need to search the place, and we'll to ask the staff questions."

"Fine," Benjamin answered, but his jaw was tight.

"We'll also need a room here, a suite if possible, with three beds. The three of us sometimes work in the middle of the night."

He knew this sounded odd, but Beth would need to share a room with them.

"Yes. Of course," Benjamin answered, seeming relieved to be back in an area where he knew exactly what to do. "The Gardenside Family Suite is available. I'll have you booked in there."

Leaning forward, Cooper said, "Thank you. If you're engaging us, we will need you to sign a contract. We can officially list tomorrow's date as our first day on the job."

To his surprise, Beth gently but quickly took the manila folder from his hand. Then she stood and reached over the desk, holding it out to Benjamin. When he took it, she brushed her hand against his.

.   .   .   .   .

Thirty minutes later, after the contract had been discussed and signed, they retrieved all their gear from the Jeep and were shown to their suite. The bellhop who escorted them took in the sight of Cooper and Lee's old boots and canvas jackets with some disdain and did not bother waiting for a tip.

Once the three of them were alone, Cooper set his pack on top of a bed, barely noticing their surroundings, but Lee whistled.

"Quite a step up from a Motel 6," he said.

"Mmmmmmm?" Cooper asked.

"So p... pretty," Beth said, looking all around.

Glancing up, Cooper took note of the two-room suite. Several walls were painted a rich shade of purple with bright white trim. Some of the walls were accented in cream wallpaper with images of lilacs. The curtains were white lace. In addition to the beds, the suite was furnished with plush chairs and dark wood tables and a writing desk.

"Nice," he said absently, but he couldn't truly appreciate any place besides home.

"How do you want to start here?" Lee asked.

Cooper had been mulling that over and not yet come to a decision. Plus, it was almost seven o'clock, and he knew Beth was probably getting hungry.

"Why don't we go down to the restaurant and have dinner," he said. "We can talk over our options while eating."

"Sounds good," Lee answered. "If our meals are covered, I'm getting a steak."

But Beth looked over at them, while standing by a table, and picked up a menu. "They have r... room ser... vice." She sounded frightened, and Cooper wondered why.

Lee did not appear to hear the apprehension in her voice and motioned for her to join them. "No. Come on. We need to get the lay of the place and get a sense of who might talk to us. We should go down to the restaurant."

Dropping her eyes, she followed them out of the room and down through the hotel to the restaurant on the ground floor. The vast dining room itself was more welcoming than Cooper had expected, in shades of rust-brown and olive green. Antique chandeliers hung from the ceiling.

As the three of them entered, Louise, the front desk attendant, followed them, but then she walked past them to a tall woman in a floor-length dress and whispered a few words. Cooper picked up, "guests of Mr. Jackson."

The tall woman nodded and smiled at Lee. "Good evening. Table for three?"

Lee smiled back. Beth kept her eyes on the floor.

A few moments later they were seated. As they looked at their menus, Beth leaned closer to Lee, pointing to something.

"That one?" Lee asked.

"Yes," she whispered.

A man in his early twenties walked up to the table. He was broad-shouldered with a chiseled jaw—and with product in his short hair.

"My name is Christophe," he said, "and I'll be taking care of you this evening. Tonight's soup is Manhattan clam chowder, and our dinner special is a walnut-crusted halibut. It's excellent. Can I start anyone with a drink? We have several microbrews on tap and an extensive wine list. I'm glad to answer any questions."

His words were smooth and practiced.

Cooper answered, "I'll take the darkest beer you have on tap."

"For me too," Lee put in.

"And for the lady?" Christophe asked.

Beth wouldn't look at him. Lee asked her, "You want lemonade?"

She nodded once, keeping her head down.

Lee looked up. "She'll have a glass of lemonade."

"We have fresh strawberry lemonade if you'd like, miss?" Christophe asked.

She wouldn't look up.

"That sounds fine," Lee answered for her. "And I think we're ready to order if that's all right."

"Of course, sir."

"I'll have the ribeye steak, medium rare, with a baked potato, and she'll have the pumpkin ravioli."

"Good choices," Christophe said and looked to Cooper. "Sir?"

"I'll have the halibut."

After an approving nod, Christophe swept away, but Cooper sat dumbfounded. "Beth, what's wrong?"

"Nothing's wrong," Lee answered for her. "She just doesn't know him. She never talks in front of people she doesn't know."

Didn't she? Cooper thought back on this and realized he'd never actually seen her speak to anyone besides himself, Lee, and Vice Principal Sanders. His already substantial concern for her increased. So... she couldn't be left home alone, and she was unable to communicate with other people without assistance?

And how had Lee noticed the latter when he hadn't?

. . . . .

After dinner, they went back to their room. Lee and Beth watched television while Cooper researched the hotel on his computer. He didn't expect to find much that might help him, but learning the history of a building was always the best place to start. The hotel had been built in 1921, and then went through a series of owners over the years. In the early 1950s, it closed down and was re-opened as a retirement home until the late 1970s. Then it was sold again, underwent a million-dollar renovation, and was reopened as a hotel. It was now recognized and protected as a national historical landmark. Both Shirley Temple and Burt Reynolds had been guests at different points in the past.

But while the place had clearly been through some financial trials, Cooper found no evidence of murder, hauntings, or even suspicious deaths.

About ten o'clock, Beth disappeared into the bathroom and came back out wearing her pajamas, which consisted of a little pink T-shirt and light gray flannel pants.

"You tired?" he asked.

"Yes."

"This way." He led her into the back room of the two-room suite. There was one queen-sized bed in this room, with two more out in the main room. "You can sleep here," he said. "Lee and I are between you and door, and you can see my bed from here. Will that be all right?"

Looking out of the room, she nodded, and he could tell from her calm expression that she meant it and wasn't just telling him what she thought he wanted to hear.

But then, she drew her phone from her pocket and began typing. He leaned over her shoulder.

The manager is hiding something. There is something he's not telling you.

Cooper digested this. "But you don't know what?" he asked quietly.

No. I only touched him for an instant, but I could feel there was something he didn't want to tell you.

"Okay. We'll talk to the staff tomorrow, and maybe we'll get an idea. I think we should start with the maid who claims she was possessed. Benjamin said she quit working here, but we can get her address."

"Yes."

Beth crawled under the covers and closed her eyes. He had a feeling she'd be asleep in minutes, so he went back out to find Lee standing near the windows, looking at the well-lit garden outside.

"This is quite a place," Lee said.

But Cooper kept thinking back to dinner, and several elements bothered him. "How did you know Beth wouldn't want to order her own food?"

"What?" Lee appeared puzzled by the question. "It has nothing to do with what she wants. She can't."

"Can't?"

"Surely you've noticed? She's sometimes a little better with women, but there's no way she could have talked to that waiter tonight."

Of course Cooper knew she had social anxiety issues, but he was suddenly uncomfortable that Lee seemed to both understand and accept the extent of these issues better than he did.

"Well..." Cooper began, "maybe you shouldn't have just ordered for her. Maybe you should have let her try to order for herself."

Turning away from the window, Lee frowned. "Then she would have gone hungry." He crossed his arms. "You're the one who said we should keep her with us because she so was damaged she couldn't function in foster care or out in the real world. I know I fought you at first, but then I saw you were right. She can't function, not without help. And that's what we both signed on for." He walked a few steps closer, his arms still crossed. "Are you regretting this?"

Was he?

"No," Cooper answered, and he meant it. "I just didn't think some of this through." Not only would they need to bring her on jobs, they would need to handle communication for her. And what would happen when they were called into a vampire hunt? She was terrified of vampires. "I guess we'll just figure things out as we go."

Lee nodded. "Good. 'Cause we're in this now, and there's no going back."

The determination in his voice surprised Cooper, but it probably shouldn't have. Lee was beyond cautious when it came to making commitments to other people, but once he was in, he was *in*.

Cooper should have remembered this.

CHAPTER EIGHT:

THE ANGRY MAN

In the middle of the night, Lee was awakened by the sound of screaming. He sat up, alert but disoriented. The screaming was not close by, but coming from somewhere outside the room, from a deep-voiced woman.

Cooper was scrambling off his bed, and Beth came hurrying through the open archway from her room. As Cooper reached the door and ran out, Lee moved to follow, but he half-turned toward Beth. Her hair hung in messy waves around her alarmed face.

"You stay here!" he ordered. "I mean it."

Then he ran out the door and into the hall, following both Cooper and the sounds of the screams. They were both wearing sweatpants and T-shirts. Their feet were bare. Down the hallway, they rounded a corner to see other guests coming out of their rooms, but Cooper didn't slow down—and neither did Lee. They dodged around any guests who didn't see them coming.

Then up ahead, a door opened and a large, heavy-set woman in a silk nightgown nearly fell out into the hallway, screaming, "Help! Help me! He's dying! I can't get him warm! Please, someone, help!"

Her back was to them, and she didn't see either of them.

Without stopping, Cooper ran into the room, with Lee right on his heels.

Both men skidded to a stop, taking in the scene before them in a matter of seconds. A balding, middle-aged man in pajamas lay on the floor choking, but the chokes were growing weak. His skin was turning blue, and his fingers curled inward.

Cooper rushed forward, grasping the man's hands. "He's freezing."

They both knew what this was. There was a ghost inside him, freezing him to death.

"Did you bring the blade?" Cooper asked wildly.

The blade.

"No!" Lee hadn't brought anything. He'd just run toward the sound. There was no time to go back and get it.

In desperation, Cooper laid the man on his back and place both hands on the man's chest. "*Ut ex spiritu. Derelinquamus.*" Leaning closer, he shouted into the man's face, "*Derelinquamus!*"

He was trying to drive out the ghost.

But the man's fingers curled further inward. His skin was turning from blue to white. Only seconds had passed, and his wife was still screaming in the hallway.

"Lee," a quiet voice said from behind him.

Whirling, he saw Beth standing there, holding out Cooper's onyx blade. Not even angry that she'd disobeyed his order, he grabbed the blade from her hand and rushed forward.

"Cooper, move!"

Dropping to his knees, Lee pressed the side of the blade against the man's face. A whooshing sounded, though Lee saw nothing, and the man on the floor gasped without opening his eyes.

The spirit was out of him. It had not allowed itself to be seen, but it was out.

Beth hurried into the bathroom, and the sound of running water followed. "Quick!" she called. "B... bring him."

She was running a hot bath.

Right at that moment, a hotel security guard and the stricken man's wife came in. The wife still appeared hysterical, but she'd stopped screaming. Cooper looked at the guard. "Help us get him into the tub. We need to warm him up."

For some reason, when Cooper spoke, people listened. The guard hurried forward to help, and Cooper said the woman, "Call 911 and get him an ambulance."

. . . . .

Less than an hour later, Cooper, Lee, and Beth were back in their room, and Cooper was trying to decide what to do.

The momentary crisis had been averted. Beth's quick thinking with the blade and then the bathtub had probably saved the man's life. Paramedics had arrived twenty minutes later, and it seemed the man would recover.

But... that still left a dangerous ghost loose in the hotel in the middle of the night. Apparently, Benjamin Jackson had gone home, but they had been assured, "The manager will be informed of the situation as soon as possible."

So much for a low profile. Half the hotel must have heard the ruckus. And what Cooper was now considering might make things worse before they got better.

"That wasn't anything like what the manager described," Lee said after closing their room door.

This was certainly true. What they'd witnessed was a typical angry spirit using its main offensive power. "I know. That ghost was trying to kill him, not possess him."

Lee glanced at Beth. "I'd prefer you to do what I tell you, but that was good thinking bringing us the blade." He shook his head. "How did you know what onyx can do? You've never seen us hunt a ghost. Sometimes, you knowing exactly what one of us needs is almost like magic."

That last statement was too close to the truth, and when Beth didn't answer, Cooper said, "She's probably heard us talking."

Lee appeared to accept this and didn't press. Instead, he asked Cooper, "What do you want to do now?"

"I think we should summon that ghost and try to handle this tonight. It's past midnight, and per the contract, we're on the clock."

"You want to try from here?"

Cooper considered this. "No. We'd have to peel up the carpet. The dining room in the restaurant has hardwood floors and more space, with four windows facing the garden. If the spirit won't let me help it cross, we can drive it outside and ward a window as fast as possible."

"Will that work long enough for us get a ward on all four directions? This place is huge."

The gardens faced east. They would need a ward on the north, south, and west sides of the hotel as well.

Beth stepped closer to Cooper and held out her phone.

While you and Lee are summoning the spirit, I can draw wards on the other three directions.

It still unsettled him how much she seemed to know. He'd never shown her how to draw a ward. "We can't put the wards up first. They affect the spirit's energy and make the summoning more difficult." He paused. "But we could place you on the west side, and if I need to drive the spirit out on the east side, I could call you on your cell... and you can start warding fast. You do the west and north side. We'll do the east and south."

"Wait a minute," Lee said in alarm. "What is she offering to do? Wait someplace by herself? Outside the circle? On the other side of the hotel from us? No. That's not happening."

Beth typed quickly and held out her phone.

I want to help. I am not afraid of ghosts.

"Well, you should be," Lee returned.

"She'll be all right," Cooper said. "I'm hoping this spirit will listen to reason and let me help it, but if not, it won't get past us, and we'll drive it outside. And you're right that this place is huge. We're going to need some help to keep it from coming back in."

Lee shook his head again. "I don't like this."

Beth touched his arm. "I w... will be f... f... fine."

Still not convinced, Lee turned to Cooper. "We don't even have a name yet. You sure you want to try already?"

Cooper wasn't sure, but they didn't have much choice if they wanted to protect the hotel's guests tonight. The problem was that he had almost nothing upon which to focus for a summoning spell. With situations like Garrett Talbot, the summoning had been almost effortless. Cooper had had strands of the man's hair. But if he even had a name and had seen a photo or knew something about the spirit, it gave him a point of focus... of connection.

As of yet, for the Colombia Gorge Hotel ghost, they had nothing.

That meant he'd need to draw on his own life energy. He'd done this only twice, and both times it had drained him badly. He'd barely been able to stand afterwards. But they'd taken on this job, and tonight, a guest of the hotel had nearly been killed, would have been killed if they hadn't reached him in time. And the ghost was still loose.

"We have to try," he said. "This can't wait."

Thankfully, the restaurant was part of the hotel and as opposed to locked doors, there was a large arched entrance. The place was closed in the middle of the night, but Cooper and Lee simply walked in and began moving tables.

There was no one else about, so they had full freedom to work alone.

Lee's expression was tense, and Cooper knew his friend was still uncertain about them sending Beth to the west side of the hotel—with a can of black spray paint—to wait for a phone call. But Beth had offered, and Cooper was certain they could protect her from here.

Once three tables had been moved to clear some space, he half-knelt down on the floor, digging through his open pack. This room had been a good choice. From experience, he knew spirits responded better when summoned inside of larger spaces. Also, much of the hotel was carpeted, and he needed a hard surface for the circle.

Lee stood close beside with the shotgun.

Using a piece of chalk, Cooper drew the circle around them both. Then he settled in the center with Lee directly behind him. Cooper took out the clear quartz crystal, brass bowl, a small knife, and a lighter. He also set his onyx blade and a can of spray paint on the floor beside him. After setting the crystal in the center of the bowl, he picked up the knife and cut a few strands of his own hair. The impetus for this summoning had to come entirely from himself. After dropping the strands of hair into the bowl, he sliced down the center of his left hand. For this summoning, he'd need more blood than his index finger could provide. He let blood drip down into the bowl and onto some of the hair, but he made sure a few strands remained dry.

Then he lit the hair on fire, crossed his legs, and closed his eyes.

He had to begin by making a connection. *"Spiritus Patris habitationem istam, exaudi me,"* he whispered, reaching out with his mind. *"Spiritus Patris habitationem istam, venerunt ad me."*

At first, he felt only emptiness, and then... he felt a presence on the edge of his awareness, and he latched on. This was the difficult part. Drawing on his own life energy, his voice rose. *"Spiritus Patris habitationem istam, venerunt ad me."*

The presence fought him, and he had nothing concrete to focus on to help with the connection, so the only thing he could do was expend more energy and not let go. *"Venerunt ad me!"*

Pulling with all the strength inside himself, he continued drawing the presence closer. A bead of sweat trickled down the side of his face from the effort, and he could feel his life energy beginning to drain.

"Coop?" Lee said from behind him, sounding worried. "You're going pale."

Ignoring him, Cooper placed both palms against the

floor, ignoring the pain from the cut on his left hand. *"Venerunt ad me!"*

Then the presence was in the dining room. He could feel it, and he switched from locating to summoning.

"Spiritus, ostende mihi te ipsum." Drawing strength from somewhere, he called loudly, *"Spiritus, ostende mihi te ipsum!"*

He opened his eyes.

The air in front of him shimmered and wavered. Then a transparent form slowly began to appear.

. . . . .

Lee had been on the verge of physically stopping Cooper when the ghost began to materialize.

From the initial outline, Lee could see they were dealing with a man, slender and of medium height. As the image sharpened, he made out brown silk pajamas and a paisley dressing robe. The man was elderly, perhaps late seventies, with hawkish features and a head full of silver hair, cut to where it made a peak at the center of his forehead. His hands were gnarled, and his knuckles were swollen. But these things registered only at the edge of Lee's awareness as his body tensed upon seeing the man's expression of rage, of mad hatred.

Rage poured off the spirit in waves.

The ghost flew toward the circle and bounced back in surprise. Then he hissed, exposing two rows of even teeth.

"It's all right," Cooper said, struggling to stand, pale and drained. "We want to help you."

The ghost looked all around the dining room. "Where is she?" He didn't shout the words, but his voice resonated with anger. "Where is Victoria?"

Lee tightened his grip on the shotgun.

Cooper ignored the question. "You're trapped between worlds. Let me help you cross over. I can help you find peace."

The ghost's upper lip curled in contempt. "Peace?" He gave a short, mean laugh and looked around again. "Where is she?"

"Let me help you cross over," Cooper repeated.

After one more glance at the chalk circle on the floor, the spirit turned and raced toward the archway, out of the restaurant. This seemed to catch Cooper off guard, but not Lee. He'd had a feeling this ghost would try to bolt.

Rushing forward, Lee left the circle and dashed around to cut the spirit off, aiming the gun and firing. The man's incorporeal image exploded and vanished.

Then he reappeared in the middle of the room.

Lee felt a moment of satisfaction at the shock on his face. Ghosts were always beyond surprised the first time they felt pain.

"Rock salt," Lee said. "Hurts, doesn't it?" Then he aimed the gun again.

Cooper moved into action in the same instant. Though still pale, he somehow managed to run forward with his onyx blade in one hand and the can of spray paint in the other. Lee and Cooper both knew that momentary shock would cause the spirit to flee through the window. This was the one thing they could always count on, that after having felt nothing for so long, the experience of pain was so frightening and disorienting, the ghost always fled in the direction they drove it.

This had never failed.

Cooper slashed the onyx blade right through the ghost's chest, and then braced as the spirit cried out and floated backwards in further shock... but it did not fly through the window to escape. Instead, the ghost stopped just out of reach and swiveled his head to see Lee striding forward with the shotgun. The sight of Lee coming with that gun—coupled with Cooper and the blade—had always caused a spirit to fly away from them.

But the man's lips curled again, and he whooshed to one side, dodging around Lee and floating deeper into the dining room.

His face shifted to rage again, and for a second, Lee thought he might charge in an attempt to enter one of them. But the man's transparent eyes dropped to the gun again, and then he whirled, flying through the dining room wall and vanishing from sight, heading deeper into the hotel.

Cooper stumbled forward in disbelief. "What just happened?"

Lee was equally stunned, but then Cooper sank to his knees, as if he could no longer remain on his feet.

Alarmed, Lee went to him quickly, dropping down, nearly forgetting about the ghost at the sight of his friend's pinched face. He could see Cooper had nearly exhausted himself. "What can I do?"

But Cooper shook his head. "Not for me. Find Beth," he breathed.

Lee went cold. The ghost was both visible and loose inside the hotel. And Beth was alone.

Still gripping the shotgun, he started running.

. . . . .

Beth waited on the far west side of the hotel, in a hallway, open spray paint can in one and her phone in the other. She would need to act quickly when Cooper called, paint her ward, and then run to paint the other one on the north side of the hotel. Earlier, before leaving for the dining room, Cooper had spent ten minutes teaching her how to draw the wards.

She was not afraid, and if anything frightened her here, it was the prospect of running into another guest of the hotel and being asked a question. But at the moment, it was nearly two o'clock in the morning, and there was no one about. She was alone.

She was glad to be useful to Cooper and Lee at last—with something besides cooking a meal they liked. She was working with them, helping them to earn their living. The thought made her happy and determined at the same time. She would not fail in her task.

Standing ready, she suddenly felt something on the edge of her awareness: anger.

It grew stronger at a rapid pace, and she was aware of the ghost even before she saw him come around the corner at the end of the long hallway. From the dis-

119

tance, she could see he'd been elderly when he died. She could see his silk pajamas and a paisley dressing gown.

He stopped at the sight of her, and she was instantly aware of two things: 1) Cooper had managed to fully summon the spirit and 2) It had escaped him. He and Lee had not driven it outside.

The ghost hung there in the air, his expression twisted with anger. She could feel waves and waves of rage pouring from him. And then... he began coming toward her.

Her mind raced, but she shifted her plan instantly. Earlier while sitting with Cooper, as he'd shown her how to draw the wards, she'd let her arm touch his, and she'd searched his thoughts through the entire lesson. There, she'd seen many wards. Some for keeping spirits out of a building, some for keeping a spirit bound, and some that would repel a ghost. Opting for the latter, she turned and swiftly drew an eye of Horus with a few smooth sprays of the can.

When she turned back, the ghost was only about ten feet away. She could clearly see his narrow, hawkish features, still almost handsome. She could see his silver hair coming to a peak high in the center of his forehead. She could see the malevolence in his blue eyes. His hands were gnarled, and the knuckles of his fingers were badly swollen.

But he'd stopped moving toward her, his eyes narrowing upon the symbol, and he began floating backwards, away from it, away from her, as she knew he would.

However, then he closed his eyes and appeared to relax, almost as if he could exhale, and his colors began to fade. Soon he disappeared from sight. But she did not move or step away from the symbol. She could still feel him, still feel his anger.

Long moments passed, and then his presence was gone. He'd cast off Cooper's summoning spell, faded from sight, and then left her alone in the hallway, but he was still somewhere in the hotel. That much she knew.

Pounding footsteps sounded, and Lee came running around the corner with the sawed-off shotgun in his hand. At the sight of her, his expression melted into relief, and he closed the distance between them in a matter of seconds.

"Are you all right?" he asked, but his eyes were on the ward she'd painted.

"Yes. The s... s... spirit was here. He is g... gone from here now, but s... still in the hotel."

Lee looked around and then back at the ward. "Did Cooper show you how to paint that one?"

"Yes."

She didn't know how else to answer. In a way, he had shown her.

Still breathing in what sounded like relief, he reached out for her. "That was good thinking. I didn't see him show you that one. I'm glad he did." Propelling her forward, he said, "We've got to get back to the dining room. He's in a bad way."

CHAPTER NINE:

THE POSSESSION

For the rest of that night, Cooper slept like the dead. When he woke to the sound of soft voices, sunlight streamed in the windows. He barely remembered Lee half-carrying him back to their room in the night and then Beth helping him into bed. Opening his eyes, he flinched slightly. His body felt as if he'd run a marathon.

Instantly, Beth was at his side, sitting on the bed, placing her hand on his forehead.

"You a... ache in your b... b... bones," she said.

He could not disagree.

"You all right?" Lee asked, walking over.

"Yeah. I will be."

Beth whisked away from his side, returning quickly with a cup of coffee. Sitting up in bed, Cooper took a few sips, savoring the warmth and rich flavor. The digital clock on the side table flashed 9:02 a.m.

"Anything else happen last night?" he asked.

"No," Lee answered. "All quiet. Maybe you drained him as much as he drained you."

Cooper didn't know. This entire situation was different from anything they'd dealt with before. "Why didn't that ghost rush away from us? It should have gone right through the window."

Lee shook his head. "I don't know. But we need to find out who he is. We can't solve much until we know who is and how he died."

"I didn't see any visible wounds."

"Me either. But did you notice his hands? What was that? Some kind of arthritis?"

"Maybe." Cooper sighed and leaned against the head-board. So far, from what they'd been told, the ghost had simply possessed people, without injuring anyone, but last night, it had gone vengeful. What could have changed? Could his behavior have changed due to their arrival?

"I don't think we'll get any help from Benjamin Jackson," he said. "That means we'll need to talk to someone who's been possessed."

On that score, they had only one lead, the maid who had claimed to be possessed and then quit her position here at the hotel. They'd need to get her information from someone at the front desk. This thought led to another.

"Did you clean up after us in the dining room?" he asked Lee.

"Yes. I even scrubbed up the chalk and put the tables back."

"Good." Cooper nodded.

There was no need for anyone to know they'd been in there—or what they had been doing.

.   .   .   .   .

After breakfast in the dining room, Cooper got the name and current address of the hotel maid: Anita Ramirez. She had an apartment in Hood River.

Heading out of the hotel, Cooper, Lee, and Beth all climbed back into the Jeep. Lee offered to drive, and Cooper let him. The address was only about seven minutes away. Though sore and weary, Cooper was starting to feel a little more like himself. Still, he was glad to let Lee drive.

Hood River was a charming town of shops and bistros. The hills all around the town were dotted with clusters of brightly painted houses amid dense ever-green trees. Lee pulled up in front of a small apartment building sporting four units.

"She lives in A-1 on the ground floor," Cooper said.

Beth climbed out first, looking around. Today, she wore the faded jeans and one of the white T-shirts she'd picked out yesterday. They suited her. Somehow, she looked more like a typical teenaged girl.

As he got out and closed the Jeep's passenger side door, Cooper pondered the best way he might get Anita to talk to them. He wished he could have called her first, but the only information he'd been able to glean from Louise (at the hotel's desk) was a name and home address.

Leading the way, he walked up to the door labeled A-1 and knocked. A few moments passed before he heard footsteps, and then the door cracked.

A small woman in her twenties peered out at them. She had dark hair and dark eyes, and her expression shifted to surprise at all three of them standing on her porch.

"Ms. Ramirez," Cooper said quickly. "Please forgive the intrusion. Benjamin Jackson from the hotel sent us over. He's hired us to assist him with the... situation there. Would you mind talking to us for a few minutes?"

Surprise turned to alarm, and shaking her head, she began to close the door. "No. I'm sorry. I don't work there anymore."

Knowing it was risky, Cooper put his hand out onto the door and stopped her from closing it. "Please. Right now, you're the only one who can help. A man was nearly killed last night."

Her gaze flew to his hand on the door and then back to his face.

"Killed?" she whispered. "How?"

"By the spirit haunting the hotel," Cooper answered bluntly. "He entered a man who nearly froze to death in a matter of seconds. The last thing I want to do is make this worse for you, but we have to learn more, and you're the only one who can help."

With her eyes still on his face, she shook her head again. "He? You think the spirit is a man? No. Victoria is a woman."

Cooper went still, not sure how to process this information. At a loss, he simply said, "Could we come in? Please."

Slowly, she stepped back and let them in, glancing uncertainly at Lee first and then down to Beth.

But Beth smiled at her and said clearly, without stammering, "It's all right. They will help."

She seemed to have no trouble speaking to Anita. Perhaps she was less inhibited with other frightened women.

They walked into a small living room with only a couch, one end table, and a television for furniture. But the adjacent dining room sported a table with four chairs.

"We can sit there," Anita said. "But I'm not sure how much I can help you."

Last night, the angry ghost had clearly stated he was looking for Victoria. As Cooper sat down across from Anita, he said, "You were possessed by a spirit? Was it Victoria?"

Anita nodded. "She... she wanted help. She was begging for help, but I was so afraid, and I didn't understand what was happening. I pushed her out, and then I ran. I quit my job. I can't go back there." She dropped her gaze to the table. "But now, I wish I had been brave enough to at least listen to her. I couldn't help her when she died, and I was too afraid to help her later. I don't know what she was afraid of."

Lee sat up. He rarely spoke during interviews, but he cut in quickly. "What do you mean you couldn't help her when she died? Did you know her?"

Anita looked up at him. "A little. She was a guest of the hotel a few weeks ago. She was an older woman, but not elderly... just alone and a little sad. She always tipped me so well for cleaning her room. But she had a heart attack, by herself in the middle of the night, and no one knew. No one was there to help her. I kept thinking that if someone had just known, we could have called an ambulance."

"And this was a few weeks back?" Cooper asked.

"Yes."

Anger rose up inside him. Benjamin Jackson had assured them there had been no recent deaths at the hotel. But how was Victoria connected to the vengeful spirit he had summoned last night?

"What was her last name?" he asked.

"Ivers," Anita answered. "Victoria Ivers."

. . . . .

"You told us there had been no recent deaths," Cooper accused.

He was facing Benjamin Jackson across the manager's desk and trying to hold his temper. Lee and Beth were both in the office as well, but they stood near the closed door.

"A heart attack is not a suspicious death," Benjamin fired back. "I assumed you were asking about suspicious deaths. And you told me you could handle this by quietly searching the hotel and speaking to some of the staff! Last night, half the hotel was woken up and we had paramedics here. Paramedics!"

"We can't help you unless you are open with us. The paramedics were here because last night, one of your guests was nearly killed, and we can't stop any of this until we understand exactly what we're dealing with."

"And how would knowing about a guest's heart attack a few weeks ago possibly help you?"

"Because according to Anita Ramirez, the spirit who entered her was Victoria Ivers."

"What?" Benjamin blinked. "Anita didn't... she didn't say anything about that."

"How could she?" Lee asked from where he stood across the office. "You said you never spoke to her."

Benjamin's eyes were shifting back and forth quickly. "Ms. Ivers? Anita gave you her name?"

"Yes," Cooper bit off, "and you need to tell us everything you know about this woman."

Regaining some of his composure, Benjamin shrugged. "We weren't well acquainted, but she was an heiress from California, family money. She could have bought and sold the rest of us. I put her in a river-side suite, but for her, I'm sure that was the equivalent of 'roughing it'. We tried to make her stay as comfortable as possible. She was only with us a few days, and then..." He trailed off.

"What was the reason for her visit?" Cooper asked.

"How should I know?" Benjamin snapped. "It is not my custom to question our guests."

Cooper stared at the man, once again feeling the urge to quit and walk out the door. If he wasn't already so invested here—and being well-paid for his time—he would have quit. But there was mystery here, and there was a dangerous presence in the hotel, and he wanted to solve this.

.   .   .   .

Back their suite, at the slender writing desk, Cooper set up his computer, connected to the hotel's Wi-Fi, and launched into research. Lee hadn't slept much the night before, so he lay down in Beth's bed in the back room for a short nap.

Beth sat beside Cooper at the desk. She kept her phone in her hands.

It didn't take long to find Victoria Ivers of Marin County, California.

"She was I... lovely," Beth said, looking at the first photograph on the computer screen.

Cooper could not disagree. The photo showed a woman in perhaps her mid-to-late thirties, with thick auburn hair swept back into a knot at the base of her head. She wore a black turtleneck and diamond earrings. Her face was slender. Her green eyes were sad.

The photo was captioned: Victoria Ivers, 1988.

"Thirty-two years ago," he said. Then he scanned the page. "She was born in 1952. Her parents were Quentin and Marie Ivers. It sounds here like the family money came from her mother's side, but her father invested heavily in Ford in the 1940s, and he made a fortune." He paused. "Her mother died of cancer when Victoria was only sixteen."

Beth's expression shifted to sympathy. "Sad."

"Yes." He kept reading. "Her father died in 1979. She inherited everything. Then she had a brief marriage beginning in 1980 to an Alfonse Garcia. They divorced in 1981, and she began working with several international charities."

He continued reading about her charity work, but nothing here told him much about her other than she was a wealthy heiress, she believed in helping others, and she had lost a number of people she cared for. Hoping he could find something useful, he continued reading until he heard Beth make a soft gasp.

Turning his head quickly, he saw her looking at her phone screen. "What is it?"

She held it up. "Quentin I... I... Ivers."

He found himself staring at a photo of a man with hawkish features, blue eyes, and his hair cut to a peak in the center of his forehead.

"That's him!"

Beth nodded. "Yes. Look." She pointed to a paragraph below the photo. It was a short biography of Victoria's father.

Quentin Ivers was born in 1901 Redding, California, to Edward and Cathleen Ivers. His father, Edward, worked as an engineer for Union Pacific Railroad. Quentin attended Stanford University, studying mathematics and finance. Later, he worked for Wells Fargo.

He did not marry until 1940, shortly after meeting Marie Van Buren at a charity ball in San Francisco. Ivers invested heavily in the Ford Motor Company, eventually serving on the board of investors. The couple remained childless for twelve years, until the birth of their daughter, Victoria, in 1952.

Ivers' wife Marie died of cancer in 1968. He died in his sleep in 1979 while residing at the Columbia Gorge Hotel during the years it had been reno-vated into a retirement home.

Cooper stared at the last line. "He died here, in the hotel."

Drawing her phone closer, Beth switched over to the note pad app and began typing. When she finished, she held it out again.

Quentin and Victoria's spirits are both here in the ho-tel, and it cannot be a coincidence that she died here a few weeks ago.

"Yes, but if Quentin died in 1979, why has he just gone vengeful now?"

We need to ask Victoria.

Cooper sighed. Of course he knew this. Victoria was the key. She was the one who had possessed Anita, begging for help. But help with what? Protection from the ghost of her father? Or maybe did she not realize she was dead and needed help crossing over?

Something else?

Cooper felt drained all the way to his bones. His left hand was still sore from where he'd cut it. He flinched at the thought of another summoning so soon. Still, there was no choice, and this time, he had both a name and an image of Victoria's face. Also, if she was pos-sessing people to ask for help, she might want to be summoned, and this would make the process easier on him.

"We'll need to wait until tonight," he said. "Full dark-ness is best for a summoning... and that will give me time to rest."

Beth nodded. Then she yawned, and he realized she'd not had much sleep the night before either.

"Do you want a nap?" he asked.

It was raining outside now, and the room felt overly cool.

She nodded and stood.

He expected her to lie down on his or Lee's bed out in the main room of the suite, but she walked toward the back room. Puzzled, Cooper followed. Lee was sound asleep, lying on his back.

Beth picked up a spare blanket and crawled onto the bed, covering herself with the blanket and curling up against Lee's left arm for warmth. Then she closed her eyes.

Cooper stood in the archway, uncertain what to do or say. In some ways, she was like a child. Her sheltered upbringing had caused some of this. But she was not a child. She was nearly a woman, and he needed to find a way to tell her that she couldn't simply crawl in bed with him or Lee if she was cold or scared.

He needed to explain this to her.

For now, he let it go and walked back out to his computer. He would explain it, but not today.

.　　.　　.　　.　　.

At nine o'clock that night, Beth helped Lee to push both beds in the main room up against the inner wall. Then they peeled up the carpet—and the carpet pad.

As she'd not been able to watch Cooper summoning Quentin Ivers last night, she watched him curiously now, interesting in knowing what he did—and how he did it. She watched as he gathered a brass bowl, a crystal, matches, a small knife, his onyx blade, and a thick piece of chalk.

He drew a large circle on the bare floor and then sat cross-legged in the middle.

Lee stepped inside the circle, carrying his shotgun, and motioned her to join him. "No matters what happens, do *not* step outside this circle. Do you understand?"

He'd never spoken to her in a tone like that before, and she detected a hint of threat in his voice.

"Yes," she answered, and she meant it. But no matter how he sounded, she would never fear Lee. She'd experienced enough of his emotions to know he was simply over-protective. His warning came from a place of concern.

Cooper set the brass bowl in front of himself and then set the crystal inside. He laid his onyx blade on the floor beside himself. Then, he picked up the small knife, and cut several strands of his own hair. Using the knife, he cut the thumb of his left hand and let blood drip down into the bowl.

He focused on the crystal for a long moment, and then lit the hair inside the bowl on fire.

"Victoria Ivers," he said softly. He closed his eyes. *"Spiritus Patris habitationem istam, venerunt ad me."* Then he sat straight, as if via a jolt of surprise, and his eyes opened instantly. *"Spiritus, ostende mihi te ipsum."*

The air before them wavered, and a transparent woman appeared. Though in her sixties, she was still lovely, with thick auburn hair, perhaps faded from time but not gray. Her eyes and mouth were lined, but the skin over her cheekbones and chin was smooth. She wore a black turtleneck and narrow skirt. She still looked very much like the photo Beth had found online.

But Beth did not focus on spirit's physical presence long, for the woman's features twisted in desperation as she held out her hands. She mouthed the word, "Help," but no sound came.

"Victoria?" Cooper said. "Do you understand that you have died? You don't belong here now. Let me help you to cross over."

Shaking her head quickly, anxiously, her gaze turned to Beth. As they locked eyes, a wall of fear and desperation hit Beth so hard she nearly stumbled.

"Victoria," Cooper said. "Can you hear what I'm saying?"

On more than one occasion, Beth had picked up from his thoughts that communication with spirits was nearly always unpredictable. Some could speak. Some could not. Some could hear him. Some could not.

Victoria's transparent green eyes held Beth's. They were begging, pleading.

Almost without thought, Beth stepped outside the circle.

"No!" Lee called.

His left hand snaked out and grabbed her wrist, pulling her back inside. His grip was like a vise.

"Lee, let g... go. It's all r... r... right."

"No," he said, aiming the shotgun at Victoria over the top of Cooper's head.

But Beth knew she had to step out. She had to reach Victoria—or let Victoria reach her.

"C... Cooper," Beth said. "Please. It's all right. She needs h... help. Please."

Still sitting, Cooper looked up at them, his face awash with indecision. Then he said, "Lee. Let go."

"What?" Lee was incredulous.

"Do it."

"No."

Turning his torso, Cooper nodded his head and repeated, "Lee. Let go."

Breathing out through his teeth, Lee suddenly released his grip, but his face was tense.

As Beth stepped outside the circle, Victoria flew to her. Quickly, Beth raised one palm. Victoria stopped, surprised now. Somehow, Beth had been able to hold her off from simply entering.

"Let me in," the ghost mouthed.

Beth lowered her hand.

"No!" Lee shouted, stepping toward them.

Beth turned her head to look at him. "It's all right," she said again.

Then Victoria was inside her, inside her body, inside her mind. An instant of terror hit, but the fear was Victoria's and not Beth's.

Show me, Beth said with her thoughts. *Show me what happened.*

And Victoria did.

CHAPTER TEN:

VICTORIA

At the age of twenty-seven, for the first time in her life, Victoria Ivers fell in love, hopelessly, wildly in love. Though her mother had been dead for eleven years, Victoria was still saddened by not being able to talk to her, to share this news.

Her mother would have understood. She would have listened.

However, Victoria had only her father then, and she barely knew him. He'd been fifty-two years old when she was born. On her eighth birthday, he had just turned sixty and seemed more a grandfather than a father. She knew he worked hard to make money, but as a child, she didn't realize that not everyone had servants to prepare meals, clean the house, and launder all the clothing.

Her father had purchased a gated mansion for his small family in Marin County, California, situated on a hilltop overlooking the exquisite Ross Valley, surrounded by twenty-five private acres. The mansion itself was a hybrid of mid-century and contemporary Japanese architecture. Victoria grew up running in the long halls or playing in the gardens inside the fenced property.

Her father was rarely home. But she had her mother, a sweet lively woman who was devoted to her husband and daughter. Victoria's mother had earned a bachelor's degree in social work and served on the boards of several international charities. Still, even with her work, she was always home when Victoria arrived from school each day at four o'clock—and she always greeted her daughter with a smile and a hug and bright chatter. Together, they would have a snack in the kitchen.

Quentin, Victoria's father, sometimes missed her birthdays, but he was home for the entire day on Thanksgiving and Christmas, and she thought them a normal, happy family.

When she was sixteen and her father was sixty-eight, her mother (twelve years his junior) was diagnosed with cancer and died two months later. It was only then that Victoria realized perhaps they had not been a normal, happy family. She assumed that with her mother gone, her father would alter his work schedule to be home more. But instead, he arranged the funeral and then flew to New York for a business meeting. He did not comfort Victoria. He did not ask her if she was all right.

He was away almost as much as before, and when he was home, he worked in his office. She felt like an orphan surrounded by servants. Somehow, she survived two years and turned eighteen. Then she went to Stanford, as her father had done. At first, he protested when she chose to major in social work, but she explained that she wished to follow in her mother's footsteps and serve on the boards of charities. Upon hearing this, he did a complete about-face and expressed approval. Many women of society were involved in the upper echelons of charity work, and Quentin had been introduced to more than one multi-millionaire at a charity soiree.

"I see," he said. "Yes. Your mother's connections were useful to me. Your husband will be fortunate if you can do the same for him."

His talk of husbands made her uncomfortable. He'd already introduced her to a few men he found suitable, all wealthy, boring workaholics who followed the stock market like a religion. Victoria had no intention of marrying a man like her father.

At first, he appeared troubled by her lack of interest, but then one evening, he said, "Perhaps it's best you are so particular. A young woman in your position cannot be too cautious."

A young woman in her position? What did that mean?

After graduation from the university, she became involved with the San Francisco Community Food Project. This organization supplied food to the poor. But as opposed to serving on a board, Victoria worked as a warehouse director, not organizing charity balls, but on actually obtaining and distributing food. Her father disapproved, but she told him, "One must start somewhere. I need to build up my résumé."

He might have fought her on this, but he was beginning to have health issues. He'd had trouble with arthritis for years, but when she was twenty-three and he was seventy-five, it became debilitating in a matter of months. His knuckles grew large, and his hands were gnarled. He had difficulty walking, even with a cane. He'd not yet retired, and it appeared he had no intention of doing so, but to him, image was everything. He viewed himself as a "self-made" man, and the image of physical strength and health was part of this image. But the truth was, he could no longer take care of his own physical needs.

And he wanted to keep this a secret.

So, he hired a young investment banker, John Danvers, to work as his personal assistant, and he made arrangements to go and live in a large hotel in Oregon that had been converted into a retirement home. It was expensive, but that hardly mattered. He would be far out of sight of any of his business or social connections, and he planned to work remotely, using his new assistant as a go-between.

He told Victoria, "I have always liked Oregon. I used to take your mother on vacations there to go boating on the river or hiking at Multnomah Falls."

Victoria could hardly imagine him doing either of these things.

He left her to manage the house and the staff, but she'd been doing most of this for years anyway. They currently employed two live-in maids, Nora and Adrienne. They employed a full-time cook, Mrs. Riordan, and a gardener, Moses Sheridan. House security was handled by a retired army ranger, Martin Sommers. He'd been with the Ivers family for over twenty years and had always been left to choose his own staff for the gates. He tended to hire skilled veterans. Victoria and her father both trusted Martin's judgment absolutely.

So now, with her father gone, Victoria's life was not altered much by his absence. It shamed her a little that she did not miss him. But how could she? She'd rarely spoken with him, much less spent time with him. Dutifully, she made arrangements to go up to Hood River and see him once a month.

Then, in 1979, she was attending a fundraiser for the San Francisco Museum of Modern Art when she walked into the impressionist wing and spotted some close friends of the family, Emily Spenser and her son, Michael. Emily had served on several boards with Victoria's mother. Victoria and Michael were about the same age and had been friends since childhood. He was a shy sort, who had majored in software engineering.

Victoria was pleased to see them both, and she smiled a greeting. But then... her gaze moved to the man standing beside them, and the smile froze on her face.

She'd never seen anyone like him. He was tall, wearing a tuxedo with a black shirt. All the men here wore tuxedos, but this man's fit him perfectly. He was slender with wide shoulders. His thick, black hair was parted to the side, and a shock of bangs hung over one eye. His dark eyes were large over an aquiline nose. The pale skin of his face was clean-shaven. He did not look like a lawyer, software engineer, or investment banker. There was something almost other-worldly about him.

He was beautiful.

Emily smiled back at her. "Darling, it's so good to see you. Come and meet Michael's new friend."

Emily was one of the few people Victoria knew who could use the term "darling" without sounding fake. Approaching the trio, Victoria could not stop a fluttering that was growing in her stomach. It was a completely foreign sensation.

"Victoria," Emily said, "this is Alfonse Garcia. He's an art historian from Spain. Michael met him a few months ago at the Berkeley City Gentlemen's Club, and we're so glad he did. Alfonse has been indispensable in planning tonight's fundraiser." She turned. "Alfonse, this is Victoria Ivers, a dear friend of our family."

He nodded his head once. "An honor."

In those two words, she could hear his lyrical accent, and she somehow managed to murmur some polite reply. She could not remember what.

"You have no champagne yet," he said. "Please. Allow me."

Moving to a waiter, he lifted a fluted glass from a tray and brought it back to her. As she accepted it from his hand, she suddenly wished she'd spent more time choosing her gown and doing her hair. Tonight, she wore her hair up, in a twist at the back of her neck and a simple white Christian Dior with spaghetti straps. She wished she had worn her hair down and opted for her black Chanel.

"Miss Ivers," he said. "The museum has brought in a Winslow Homer painting, on loan from New York. I should like your opinion."

He offered his arm.

Victoria knew little about art, but without hesitation, she took his arm.

That was how it started, and events moved swiftly from there. The following night, he took her to dinner, and they talked until the restaurant closed. He asked her questions about herself, about her thoughts and her life, and he listened to the answers. She'd not had this since her mother died, and she felt like a woman dying of thirst who had been handed a glass of cool water.

She could not drink enough of him.

When she was with him, she did not feel alone.

They had dinner out twice more and then went to the symphony. She knew people were talking and speculating about them, but none of that mattered. When she spoke, Alfonse listened... and he cared. She asked him questions about himself, and he gave her answers for anything she asked. He was thirty-five. He'd grown up in Spain. He worked as a consultant for the El Prado art museum in Madrid, and he was in the States doing research for a paper he was writing on the influence and contributions of American impres-sionists. He had rented a furnished apartment in San Francisco.

Outside of that, he shared little about his own life, but Victoria didn't mind. Each moment they spent together, she rejoiced in his company. He made her feel as if she were the only person in the world.

The first difficult moment occurred when she invited him to have dinner with her at the mansion. She'd let the security director, Martin Sommers, know he was coming, so he was quickly passed through the front gates. But still, when Alfonse entered the house and looked around, his pale face was nearly white.

"What is it?" she asked in alarm.

He seemed almost unable to answer and then said, "I did not... I did not quite understand."

She shook her head. "Understand what?"

He gathered his composure. "I knew you were part of society here, but I did not realize..." He trailed off, still looking around at the house foyer and into the main living area of the center wing.

Oh. It's the money.

He'd not been made aware of the extent of her fa-ther's fortune. Victoria rarely thought about money. She knew her father had set up a trust fund for her, but most young people of her set had trust funds.

"This is my father's house," she rushed to say. "Really. I just live here and manage it for him."

He looked at her, his dark eyes poring over her face. "Both my parents are dead. I have already inherited anything that I will inherit. My inheritance sustains my research and my living expenses, but I fear should anything deeper happen between us, we would not be on equal terms."

Victoria felt a chill. Her father's money had never once seemed a deficit, but now suddenly, it was. The difference in their economic status was giving Alfonse pause.

"I majored in social work," she said desperately, and then gestured around at the house. "None of this matters to me. My father has been parading wealthy investment bankers in front of me for years, but I've never wanted to be with anyone until I met you."

His eyes softened. "Truly?"

"Yes."

He kissed her mouth. It was the first time he'd done more than kiss her cheek goodnight. Feeling unsteady on her feet, she clutched his arm for support.

They did not eat dinner until after midnight.

In the weeks that followed, her need for him only grew. When he asked her to marry him, she wept because she could not imagine being so happy. She liked to envision them as simply two people who had fallen in love and were planning a normal life together.

This image was shattered when she called her father to give him the news.

"Getting married?" he said. "Married? Don't be absurd. Who is he?"

When she tried to explain that she'd known Alfonse for less than two months, and that he was an art consultant from Spain, her father's voice went cold.

"Get me all the information you can. I'll have him checked."

"I'll not have you embarrass him! He is already uncomfortable by the difference in our situations. Can you not trust that he makes me happy? Isn't that enough?"

"No."

She did not provide him with a shred of information, but it didn't matter. A week later, John Danvers, her father's assistant, called her at home, just as she was about to eat dinner. Alfonse was at his apartment tonight, working on his paper.

"Miss Ivers? It's John Danvers." He sounded hesitant.

"Yes, John. Is Father all right?"

"He's well, but he asked me to look into something and then to call you both with my findings. I just got off the phone with him."

Victoria was instantly on guard. She did not like the sound of this.

"I spoke with your friend, Michael Spenser," John said, "to get a little information on Alfonse Garcia, and then I had a background check run. It appears Mr. Garcia changed his name in 1975. Before that, he was Mateo Hernandez. He was born in Venezuela, and we could not find any record of him having ever lived or studied art in Spain. We cannot find a record of any employment whatsoever. He was married in 1971, to a Venezuelan woman, and divorced in 1975." John paused. "I am sorry to tell you these things. But your father is concerned. It seems that Mr. Garcia has not been entirely truthful with you about himself."

Victoria gripped the phone. It couldn't be true. John Danvers must have used the name Alfonse Garcia and somehow investigated the wrong man. This was a simple misunderstanding.

Without even saying goodbye, she hung up the phone. Then she called down to the kitchen phone and canceled her dinner. There was no way she could eat anything until she'd seen Alfonse.

After hurrying to the garage, she drove her Mercedes across the Golden Gate Bridge and into the city. Alfonse had rented a small, furnished apartment near Chinatown. She'd been there only once, and it had felt rather like a hotel room, but it suited his purposes well, as originally, he'd only come here to conduct research.

There was a small desk for his typewriter. He kept blank paper, his notebooks, and a stack of art books beside the typewriter.

Moments after she knocked on his door, he opened it and looked out. His expression shifted to surprise. "Victoria. I thought we were both eating at home tonight."

He wore jeans and a cream cable knit sweater. The shock of dark hair hung over his left eye. As always, she was astonished by his almost unbelievably handsome face.

"Yes... I..." She wasn't certain how to begin.

Stepping back, he let her inside. Somehow, she began to tell him the story John Danvers had told her over the phone, making it all sound as if there had been a mistake. While she spoke, Alfonse walked over and looked out the window. His frame was awash in the soft yellow San Francisco light.

When she finished, she waited for his assurances, for him to tell her that of course John Danvers had simply investigated another man.

But Alfonse was quiet for almost thirty seconds.

"Oh, Victoria." He ran a hand over his face. "I've been trying to find a way to tell you. It's all true. Everything your Mr. Danvers told you. It's true. I've never even been to Spain."

She stood there, numb, feeling nothing at all yet.

He turned toward her, away from the window. "I lied to get into the Berkeley Gentlemen's Club. I do have some family money, and I have studied art history for years on my own. It is my passion, but I am self-taught. I created the story of the Spanish art historian, consultant to El Prado, to make connections with people like the Spensers. I *am* writing a paper on the contributions of American impressionists, and I hope to publish. Through the Spensers, I've been given access to artists and scholars who would have never even spoken to me." He took a step closer to her. "I never meant any harm, and I never planned on meeting you."

As his words began to sink in, she whispered, "What about your wife?"

He shook his head. "I was young. We fell in love, but we were not suited. Stupid, young love. We parted ways. It was nothing like what you and I have. I know I should have told you, but I was afraid."

He took another step closer. "Victoria, I am so sorry. I should have told you everything before asking you to marry me... but I let myself get lost in the dream and did not think of the consequences. I began to see myself as the Spanish art historian who had won the hand of the beautiful Victoria Ivers." He glanced away. "I was a fool."

Every logical voice inside Victoria told her to turn around, leave this apartment, and drive home. But what he was saying touched her deeply. He hadn't lied in order to become part of her life. He'd lied to gain access into the art world. And then, he'd met her afterward, and he could not tell her the truth or risk losing her.

"I've lost you, haven't I?" he asked.

But when she looked at him, she saw the same person he'd been an hour ago. He was still Alfonse, a brilliant, kind man who knew how to listen. What were her options here? To break with him and leave and never see him again? Or to try to get past this, learn *all* of the real truth about him, and move onward with him as a part of her life?

"Perhaps not," she said. "But we must be truthful with each other from now on."

In three long strides, he closed the distance between them, pulling her against himself. "Truly? You could forgive me."

It seemed she had little choice. She could not even image a life without him now.

She spent half the night in his bed, in his arms. At midnight, they got up, made scrambled eggs for a late dinner, and drank crisp white wine. She didn't care who he was. She'd never known such intimacy as this, and she would not give it up.

She would not give him up.

The following day, she called her father and told him she was going to marry Alfonse.

She had no idea how he would react, but she was twenty-seven years old, and her father had little say in her life decisions. Even so, he managed to shock her.

"If you marry him," he said coldly, "you are disinherited. You won't inherit the house, and I'll have you removed from the property. I'll have your trust fund dissolved. I'll take your name out of my will. If you marry him, you will live on whatever the two of you can earn." He paused. "Tell him that."

Her hand shook. She could barely believe what he was saying.

But somehow, she managed to answer calmly, "I will."

That night, Alfonse came to the house. She took him out on the veranda overlooking the hill, and one of the maids, Adrienne, brought out a bottle of red wine with two glasses.

Once Victoria and Alfonse were alone, she poured the wine and then told him everything her father had threatened. She fully expected him to shrug and say the money and the house and the servants didn't matter, but there was always a small chance that they *did* matter. Her father had managed to create just a hint of doubt, and she awaited Alfonse's response.

Just as her father had surprised her, so did Alfonse.

He sat straight, his expression intense. "So, if you marry me, your father will impoverish you? Punish you? You would lose your home, your family, your money, your place in society, everything? Because of me?"

"I'd still have you," she answered. "That's all I want."

"No." He shook his head adamantly. "You say that now. But you don't know of what you speak. I do know." Setting his glass down, he stood. "I don't care about your father's money, but I love you." He paused and then repeated, "I love you, and I will not be the cause of your destruction."

To her shock, he began walking toward the glass doors back into the house.

"Where are you going?" she cried.

"Away. I will not do this to you. I will not be the cause of this."

She ran around him, stopping him with her hands on his chest. "Alfonse, no! I'll talk to him. I'll go to Oregon and speak with him. I'll get him to change his mind. If I can do that, will you stay?"

Alfonse's face shone with pain. "I don't want to leave. I want to spend the rest of my life with you, but I won't ruin you in the process. If you were in my place, would you ruin me?"

In truth, she would have done anything to marry him, but she didn't say that. She understood his feelings, and she believed him when he'd said he'd leave her rather than impoverish her.

In her mind, she began planning how to approach her father. She ran scenarios of his reactions over and over, as she tried to consolidate the exact right thing to say. The problem was that the more she considered this, the more she realized he would never change his mind.

As soon as she told him Alfonse would not marry her if she was disinherited, her father would pounce—even after she explained Alfonse's reasons why. How could she convince her father that Alfonse was no fortune hunter, that his reasons were honorable, born purely out of concern for her?

But the more she pondered this, the more she believed she could not convince him.

Quentin Ivers was not capable of understanding.

So, what was Victoria to do? She couldn't lose Alfonse. Slowly, almost unconsciously, a plan began taking shape.

She arranged for a plane ticket for the next day, and then she spent the night with Alfonse in her bed. At three in the morning, she slipped out of her room, left him sleeping, and went into her own bathroom to check the medicine cabinet. Some six months back, she'd had trouble sleeping and their family doctor (who made house calls) had prescribed a bottle of sleeping pills. Her father had always been one to employ doctors who were easy with a prescription pad. But after taking one of the pills, she'd stopped, as they seemed strong enough to put a horse into a coma.

Now, though, she was glad she'd kept the pills. After pocketing the bottle, she walked all the way to the servants' quarters in the east wing. Last year, Nora had been out walking the grounds on her afternoon off, and she'd slipped and badly twisted her left ankle. Victoria had called their family doctor and then allowed Nora to recover here at the house. But Nora's pain had been severe, and the doctor had left a good supply of morphine.

Nora and Adrienne shared a bathroom. Victoria had never gone inside, but she knew where it was located.

Silently, she entered the bathroom and began to search the medicine cabinet. She found nothing of use there, but she knelt to search the cupboard below the sink. It did not take long for her to find two large vials of morphine and two sterilized syringes. She pocketed both vials and one syringe.

Going back to her room, she hid the pills, morphine, and syringe in her suitcase. Alfonse slept quietly in her bed. Crawling in beside him, she drank in the sight of his face. She could not lose him.

The next day, she kissed him goodbye and took a flight to Portland. From there, she arranged a taxi to drive her to Hood River to what had once been the Columbia Gorge Hotel. Stepping from her taxi, as always, she could not help admiring her father's choice. Over the past few years, she'd come to visit him here a number of times, and from the start, she had appreciated the lines of the mission style construction and the tan stucco exterior. The view of the Columbia River below was unparalleled. Her father had always exhibited good taste.

The refurbished retirement home sported forty rooms, and her father lived in what had once been a suite on the river side, room 22. The administration kept three rooms available for visiting family members, and Victoria always stayed in one of those rooms when she visited.

After settling in, she went straight to her father's room. On the flight up, she had begun to allow herself to hope that perhaps she had been wrong. Perhaps if she spoke from her heart and explained the truth to him, her father might begin to see that her future, her happiness for the rest of her life, depended on sharing that life with Alfonse. Surely on some level, her father loved her? Surely he would want her to be happy.

Knocking lightly on the door of Room 22, she called, "Father?"

"Come."

Though his arthritis had worsened, and he now had trouble even picking up a glass, his voice was still strong. His mind was still strong.

Bracing herself, she opened the door and walked in. He sat in a chair by the window, dressed in a button-down shirt, slacks, and slippers. When she entered, he watched her carefully.

"I hope you haven't come to make a fool of yourself," he said instantly.

"I suppose that depends on what you mean."

"Well, since you're here, I assume you haven't run off with that con man and married him."

"No. I haven't."

His blue eyes narrowed. "But you haven't sent him packing?"

"No, Father. But you don't understand. The money doesn't matter to him. He lied about his credentials to become better connected the San Francisco art world for a paper he's writing. He had no idea he would meet me."

Her father laughed once. It was an ugly sound. "No idea? He'd probably been researching you for months, maybe longer. Who'd you meet him through, Harriet Charleston? Emily Spenser?"

Victoria wavered. She'd not told him that Emily Spenser had introduced her to Alfonse.

But she pressed on. "The money doesn't matter to him," she said again. "He didn't even know about it when we met. The first time he saw the house he nearly broke off with me."

"You are a fool if you believe that. What did he say when you told him you'd be disinherited?"

"He won't ruin me. He said he won't be the cause of my destruction."

At this, her father nodded in what almost appeared appreciation. "Oh. That's quite good. A good approach. And I assume you believed him?"

She stared at him. This was pointless. He had made up his mind and nothing would change it.

"Listen to me," he went on. "I meant what I said yesterday. If you marry him, I'll have you removed from the house. I'll have your checking account seized. I'll have all your credit canceled. You will have nothing."

"Do you love me at all?"

"I've worked all my life, and I won't see everything I've earned go to some lazy fortune hunter."

The last vestige of hope died. Turning, Victoria walked from the room.

∙　　∙　　∙　　∙　　∙

She waited until eight-thirty that night. Then she took pills and morphine and went back to his room. Along the way, she passed a nurse's cart and took a small paper cup the nurses used to administer pills.

She put two of the sleeping pills into the cup. Then she put the pill bottle, the vials of morphine, and the syringe into the pocket of her cardigan sweater.

This time, she didn't knock on his door, but just walked in. He was in his silk pajamas and dressing gown now. An aide was putting him into bed. Victoria waited.

When the aide had him settled, Victoria smiled at her. "I'll sit with him for a little while."

The aide left and Victoria's father watched her from his bed. She sighed and moved to join him, sitting on the edge.

"I don't want to fight any more," she said. "Just tell me what you want me to do."

"Get rid of him. And if he gives you any trouble, you tell Martin. He'll know what to do."

Victoria had sometimes wondered about their security director, Martin Sommers. Clearly, her father had hired him all those years ago for a reason. Perhaps he had more skills than running a security gate.

"All right," Victoria said, sounding conciliatory. Then she held out the paper cup with the two pills. "The nurse asked me to give you these, to help with the pain."

Whether he was aware of it or not, she had observed certain behaviors from her father over the years, and one of the things she'd noted was that if a doctor or nurse handed him pills, he took them without question.

Even so... five or six pills might have given him pause. Two pills would not.

Nodding, he took both pills, and she handed him a glass of water.

"Sleep now," she said. "You need to rest."

Searching her face with his eyes, he said, "Whether you believe me or not, I am looking out for you. I am protecting you."

"I know, Father. Let me sit with you a while."

He closed his eyes. Within moments, he was asleep, but she waited an hour. One of those pills had caused her to fall unconscious for nine hours. Two pills would put him completely under.

When she was certain that nothing would wake him, she drew the morphine and syringe from her pocket. She had seen this type of injection before, and she knew what to do. She filled the syringe with as much morphine as it would hold. Pushing up his sleeve, she found a vein and she slowly, carefully injected him with enough morphine to kill a man.

Her gaze moved to his hand, and there she saw the ring he still wore—his wedding ring. It was odd for a man's wedding ring. Silver with a small sapphire stone. Her thoughts were blurred, unclear, but suddenly, she wanted something to remind her of his connection to her mother, proof they had once been a happy family and that her father and mother had been connected. She tried to take the ring from his finger, but his knuckle was now too large. Going in the bathroom, she soaped up her hands and then went back. This time, via the soap, the ring slipped off. She put it in her pocket.

Then, she lowered his sleeve, and covered him.

Just as she finished and put the paper cup, the vials, and the needle back into her pocket, the door opened, and the aide returned.

Victoria smiled and put her finger to her lips. "He's asleep," she whispered.

Her father's chest rose and fell.

The aide smiled back and came over quietly. "Do you need anything, miss?"

"No. I think I'll go to bed now. I'll see him in the morning."

Although she'd been startled by the arrival of the aide, this could not have worked out better. Now, Victoria was no longer the last person to have seen him alive.

Quentin Ivers died in his sleep that night. The official cause of death was listed as "respiratory failure." This was a common cause listed for people who died in retirement homes.

Victoria endured the outpouring of sympathy from friends and her father's business associates. She played the part of the mourning daughter by not allowing herself to think on how he'd actually died, and by allowing herself to believe she was the mourning daughter.

When the will was read, she inherited nearly everything: the house, fifty-seven million dollars in investments; and the ten million in her trust fund was now in her name only. No one could dissolve it or take it away. Her father did leave a generous retirement stipend for both Martin Sommers, their security director, and their cook, Mrs. Riordan, as both had been loyal members of the house for years.

A month following his funeral, Victoria and Alfonse were married in a quiet ceremony at City Hall. Alfonse's face glowed with love when he spoke his vows, and she could not imagine being this happy.

She took his name and became Victoria Garcia.

And yet after the ceremony, on way down the stairs out of City Hall, she was hit by a single thought.

You are a murderer. You murdered your father.

Breathing in quickly, she pushed the thought away. He'd given her no choice.

When several family friends expressed surprise that she'd not wanted a wedding, it made perfect sense for her to respond that she and Alfonse wished to be married, but so soon after her father's death, she was not ready for a big public display.

People understood this. But Emily Spenser insisted on at least publishing an announcement in the paper, with a photo of them. She said that much had to be done, and Victoria did not object. She never mentioned this to Alfonse, but she knew he wouldn't mind.

The first four months of the marriage was the most joyous time of her life. Alfonse doted on her. They didn't even bother with a formal honeymoon because they were so happy together at the house. She took a leave of absence from her work at the community food project in order to spend her time at home. They ate all their meals together, took long walks on the grounds, and whispered their hopes and dreams to each other. He told her that he'd set up an office in the west wing, with his typewriter and books, to work on his paper. But he asked her not to visit or go in, that it needed to be his private space for work. She understood this.

Only a few things troubled Victoria.

First, she was somewhat taken aback by his manner with the servants. Victoria and her father had always treated the servants as valued employees. They'd called her Miss Ivers and him Mr. Ivers. Now, they called her Mrs. Garcia.

But Alfonse insisted they call him "sir" and not look him directly in the eyes. His manner bordered on rude. He ordered them about and then snapped if one of them displeased him. One morning, as Victoria was coming into the informal dining room for breakfast, she heard him speaking to Nora.

"Take this back at once! Tell the cook that when I order my eggs scrambled soft, I mean it. And I want a proper breakfast in front of me in ten minutes!"

"Yes, sir."

Nora scurried from the dining room, carrying a plate. She did not see Victoria and ran toward the kitchen.

When Victoria entered the dining room, Alfonse was sipping coffee and reading the newspaper. He wore silk pajamas and a dressing robe, as if he'd lived in a mansion and ordered servants about all of his life.

He smiled at her. "My love."

She decided not to mention his harsh words to Nora.

The second thing that troubled her occurred about four months into the marriage when he was ready to move back into doing serious research on his paper. He began spending more and more time away from home, sometimes even spending the night at a hotel in the city when he'd been working late interviewing a local academic. Then he mentioned that he needed access to a little spending money. All of his bills were paid by Victoria's accountant, and he'd been given a credit line with several tailors. She assumed he could handle minor expenses with his own inheritance.

But he shook his head with some embarrassment. "I am ashamed to say, but that money is gone. My travel costs here and then rent on the apartment took up my funds. In fact, I've incurred a few small debts in my research, and I need to pay my dues at the club. Once I've published my paper, more doors should be open for me. I'm hoping to find work in San Francisco at one of the art galleries." He paused. "But for now, I need to pay for parking downtown or lunch out or library fees."

What he said made sense, and she knew what high hopes he had upon publishing his paper. She simply hadn't realized his inheritance was gone.

The problem was the brunt of the money was tied up in investments. The most easily accessible money was her trust fund, most of which was liquid cash earning basic interest, in case she should ever need it. Of course she wanted Alfonse to have access to spending money for his research.

In the end, she spoke with one of her bankers and had a checking account in Alfonse's name attached to the trust. That way, he could draw money when necessary—without having to ask her. When she told him, he kissed her deeply and whispered words of gratitude. He didn't leave her side for three days.

But after that, his absences grew more frequent. He'd used some of his new expense money to acquire a full membership at Berkeley Gentlemen's Club. He said he could work there more easily than he could at home.

She grew lonely... perhaps more than lonely. He was like a drug she had come to need.

Though Victoria didn't like to complain, one night, he called from the club to say he would not be home for dinner. He'd promised to be home, and she'd dressed carefully for the evening. Mrs. Riordan was making lobster and Caesar salad. Victoria could not hold back.

"What do you mean you're not coming home?" Her voice sounded shrill to her ears. "You promised!"

The line was quiet for a moment, and then he said, "Of course I will come if you insist."

She wanted to weep. "I don't insist. But I miss you."

"I'm working."

"Yes."

This went on for three months. She was only happy when he came home. She knew she should go back to work, but instead, she gave her notice. How could she work when she might be away from the house if he came home?

She opened bottles of wine in the evening, hoping to share them if he returned, but more often than not, she drank them alone.

One night, the phone rang and instead of waiting for one of the servants to get it, she grabbed it up herself. "Alfonse?"

"No, darling. It's me." Emily Spenser's voice came from the earpiece.

"Oh, Emily." Victoria gathered herself. She'd already had two glasses of wine. "Is everything all right?"

"Yes. Fine. But I wanted to check on you." Emily sounded odd, hesitant.

"Check on me? Why?"

"Well, we haven't seen much of you, and Michael has been rather worried about Alfonse." She paused. "I know people of our set don't often speak of such things, but I wanted to tell you that Michael's father had a gambling problem."

"I am sorry. I didn't know."

"Not many people did, but if you ever want to talk, I'm here. Trust me. I will understand."

Victoria blinked. "Talk? About what?"

"About... do you mean to tell me you don't know? Oh, Victoria. I didn't realize. I should not have called." Now, Emily sounded positively mortified.

"What are you saying?"

"Nothing. I should go, my dear."

"Emily, don't hang up! What are you trying to tell me?"

A moment of silence followed. "Michael says Alfonse has been losing rather a lot at cards, at the club. Last night, he lost about twenty thousand. Oh, Victoria. I did not call to tell you this. I thought you knew."

Victoria couldn't even find the words to respond.

"My dear," Emily rushed on, sounding distressed now. "When Alfonse asked us for an introduction, I didn't think anything of it. A number of people have asked to meet you over the years. It was only afterwards that I worried. We knew so little about him."

"Alfonse asked you for an introduction?"

"Yes. Didn't he tell you? Michael arranged for his invitation to the fundraiser at the museum that night. We knew you'd be there."

Victoria hung up.

Alfonse had known about her before the night they met. How much had he known?

Now, he was playing cards at the club and losing money? Where was he getting the money? Then she knew. He was drawing it from her trust fund. Sinking into a chair, she finished the bottle of wine. What should she do? Should she call the club and insist he come home?

No. She was drunk. It would be better to wait until she could face him sober and in the daylight. Perhaps Michael was exaggerating? It was possible Alfonse had gotten dragged into one or two card games and hadn't known what he was doing. And it wasn't unexpected that he might have heard her name before meeting her. She would ask him about this.

She would need to learn the details.

For now, she went to bed.

The next morning, she woke up with a resolution. She would confront Alfonse, ask him about the gambling, and make it clear that some changes were in order. She knew his research was important to him, but wasn't she important? He would need to explain the gambling debts—but that could not be nearly as serious as Emily had suggested. This was merely a catalyst to discussing deeper issues. If he could take time away from his research to gamble, he could certainly make time for his wife.

He needed to start putting his wife first. Victoria drew a breath. Yes. Really. She should thank Emily later.

It was time to confront Alfonse.

As she walked into the dining room, she found Adrienne setting up the morning coffee.

"Good morning, Adrienne. Did Mr. Garcia come in last night?"

"Yes, Mrs. Garcia. He's in the blue guest room."

He'd taken to doing that when he came in late. He said he didn't want to disturb her.

"Should I wake him?" Adrienne asked.

"No. Let him sleep."

She wanted him fully refreshed for their discussion. Feeling better than she had in months, she was pouring a cup of coffee when the foyer phone rang. A moment later, Adrienne came back to the dining room.

"There is a Ms. Gabriela Alvarez on the phone. She says she is calling long distance. Will you speak with her?"

Victoria did not know a Gabriela Alvarez, but she rose and walked to foyer.

"Yes? Hello?"

"You were Victoria Ivers?" a woman asked. She had a lovely, lyrical accent that sounded similar to Alfonse's. "You married a man who goes by Alfonse Garcia."

A chill passed through Victoria. "How can I help you?"

"You can help yourself," the woman said. "Did you know your husband is sought for arrest in Caracas, Venezuela? I knew he'd changed his name, but I had no idea he'd gone to America until a friend sent me your wedding announcement from a San Francisco newspaper. I saw the photo. He's not aged a day."

Victoria wanted to hang up. She wanted to slam the phone down and pretend this woman had never called.

"Who are you?" she asked.

"Me? I was his wife. He's twenty years younger than me, but I believed everything he said. He took what would amount to a half million American dollars from my account, and he vanished. I had to file for a divorce that would go through if uncontested, but I filed a report with the police first." Her voice lowered. "I just called to tell you, look out for yourself."

The line went dead.

Victoria stood staring at the receiver. Then slowly, she hung up the phone and walked back to the dining room.

It couldn't be true.

If it was true, then her father had been right all along. And she had murdered him. Another thought occurred. For all John Danvers's sleuthing and all the information he'd dredged up on Alfonse, he hadn't found out about the arrest warrant in Venezuela. That piece of news might have been useful sooner.

Perhaps a half hour passed, and she had not moved. Then she heard footsteps, and Alfonse walked into the dining room, dressed for the day in black slacks and a crisp white shirt.

"My love," he said, walking toward the coffee service.

"Emily Spenser called last night."

"Did she? Is she well?"

"She said Michael is worried about your gambling debts. He says you lost at least twenty thousand the other night."

He froze with his back to her. When he turned around, she tried to read his expression. It was tight, calculated.

"Emily told you that?"

"Is it true?"

"Yes. Apparently, I am not as skilled at cards as I thought."

"She says it's not the first time." When he didn't answer, she asked, "How are you paying the debts? With money from my trust?"

His expression shifted to sorrow and regret. "I am so sorry, my love. I thought working on my notes at the club would be best, but I was drawn into a few card games, and I lost. I had to cover the debts. I hoped to find a way to put the money back before you noticed it was missing. But if Michael or Emily have suggested that my playing cards was more than a few lapses of judgment, they are not to be taken seriously."

He's lying, she thought. How had she not seen this before? He would say anything to make her forgive him.

If he had taken a half million dollars from his first wife, he'd burned through the money in a matter of four years.

"What about Gabriela Alvarez?" she asked. "Is she to be taken seriously?"

Like lightning, his features shifted, and his dark eyes flattened. He took two steps closer to her, and for the first time, she was afraid of him.

"What do you know of Gabriela Alvarez?"

"She phoned this morning. She saw our marriage photo in the paper. She told me that she is twenty years older than you. So much for young love. She told me you stole a half million dollars from her. She told me you cannot return home because there is a warrant out for your arrest."

He stared at her for a long moment. Then he started for the front door.

Nearly to the foyer, he stopped. When he looked back, his eyes had changed. This time, they were cold and almost resigned. "I did love you. In my own way I did. When we married, I even thought... I thought you to be different, that perhaps I could make a life here. But soon, I saw you had expectations of me, just like everyone else. You're all the same, all filled with expectations." He turned away again. "Goodbye."

This sounded so final that her heart jumped inside of her chest. What did he mean?

But when he walked out the door, she didn't follow or even try to stop him. She didn't know what to do. Then she went through the glass doors out onto the veranda, and she looked out over the hill at the view. Her father had been right about Alfonse. He probably had researched everything about her, down to the penny she was worth before the night they met.

And she had murdered her father.

An hour slipped past, maybe two, and she didn't move. She couldn't.

What was she going to do? Divorce Alfonse? The thought made her ill. How could she live without him, but what choice did she have? They would at least need a separation. That thought made her feel better. Yes. A separation until she could figure some things out. She'd need to arrange someplace for him to live for a while.

Reaching out, she touched the buzzer on the wall. "Adrienne, could you please come to the dining room?"

A moment later, Adrienne appeared.

"Yes, Mrs. Garcia?"

"Mr. Garcia will be away for a few weeks, and he'll need the things from his study. Could you please have them packed?"

"From his study?" Adrienne sounded puzzled.

"Yes, in the west wing. He'll need his typewriter, notes, and all of his art books."

"I'm not aware of any study. I believe his typewriter is in the closet of the blue guest room. I don't know about any books or notes."

Victoria didn't understand. She'd seen all of his beloved books scattered about at his apartment—and his notes and typewriter.

"He never set up an office in the west wing?"

"No, Mrs. Garcia."

That was impossible. Victoria strode past her, down the hall past their bedroom to the blue guest room (named for the shades of the walls, carpets, and artwork). Going to the closet, she jerked open the door. He kept all his clothes in their room, but up at the top of the closet, she saw his typewriter, still in the case, with dust on top, as if it hadn't been opened in months. There was a stack of blank paper beside it. There were no books.

Alfonse had never been working on a paper. Even this had been an illusion.

She knew nothing about her husband except that he was a liar and it appeared he'd taken his last wife for a half million dollars. This thought brought fear to her throat, and she ran from the room back to her own bedroom—which contained the closest telephone.

Quickly, she rang the bank that held her trust fund.

"Yes," she said when someone answered. "This is Victoria Garcia. Can you please tell me the balance of my fund?"

"Yes, Mrs. Garcia. Please give me a moment."

Victoria waited, tense, until the voice came back on the line.

"The balance for that account is zero. Much of the money had already been moved, but it appears Mr. Garcia had the remaining funds transferred about an hour ago. Is there a problem?"

Victoria closed her eyes. Ten million dollars. And she was the one who'd given him access to her account.

It took a few days for her to truly grasp that when Alfonse had said goodbye, it was goodbye. She never saw him again. She believed he'd meant to stay with her longer, but when he realized she'd learned the truth about his previous wife and his arrest warrant, it was time to cut and run.

So, he'd settled for ten million and he'd vanished. She did not call the police or press charges of any kind. After all, she was a murderer. Who was she to judge?

She did have one of the family lawyers arrange for a divorce that would finalize in six months if uncontested, and she changed her name back to Ivers. That was the least she could do for her father.

Once this was done, she did not leave the house for nearly a year. Alfonse may have taken millions, but the bulk of the money was still intact. She had some stocks sold and simply restructured her father's fortune. But she remained at home. She had no desire to leave the house. She longed for Alfonse and despaired of his loss and did not know how to stop the pain. She mourned him. She longed to sit on the veranda and drink white wine and share little secrets about hopes and dreams with him. She longed to sleep in his arms and wake up looking at his face.

She mourned.

But she was also plagued by guilt and regret, and in her dreams, she saw herself slipping a needle into her father's arm. Some days, she thought she was going mad.

Almost a year to the day after Alfonse vanished, Emily Spenser called to tell her there was an open seat on the board of the Task Force for Global Heath.

"We need someone like you," Emily said, "someone who actually understands the great need."

Though ten minutes before, Victoria would not have thought it possible, she suddenly found herself wanting to take the seat, wanting to do something to make up for the harm she'd done.

"Let's have lunch tomorrow, and we'll discuss it," she heard herself saying.

"I'm so glad."

This was the beginning of the next phase of her life. She never dated. She never married again. She lived a life of service, of doing all she could to help others. Years passed and then decades.

But for some reason she could not explain, instead of fading with time, her guilt over having murdered her father grew worse. In her mid-sixties, she began having heart trouble. The doctor said it was stress. In her sixty-eighth year, the guilt had become so crushing she felt she had to do something. She had to somehow put her father to rest.

Though she'd not looked at it in years, she went to her room and found his wedding ring where she'd hidden it in a drawer. It was all she had left of him—something that had been a part of him.

Almost without thinking, she made a reservation at the Columbia Gorge Hotel, which had long been turned from a retirement home back into a hotel. She reserved two rooms, one for herself, and she reserved Room 22.

Then she flew to Oregon and took a taxi to Hood River.

Everyone at the hotel was very gracious, and no one mentioned the oddity of her having reserved two rooms when she arrived alone. For several days, she could not bring herself to even enter Room 22.

She walked in the gardens. She ate in the restaurant. She sat in her room. She was trying to gather herself for a symbolic funeral. She thought that if she had a quiet ceremony, just herself, in the room where her father died, then perhaps she could find a modicum of peace.

There was a small maid with kind eyes named Anita. She took special care in seeing to Victoria's room and sometimes even asked, "Ma'am, is there anything I can bring for you?" Somehow, she seemed to understand that Victoria was here for a reason.

Victoria tipped her well.

Finally, on the third night of her stay, Victoria took her father's wedding ring and went to Room 22. For some reason, in her mind, it should have looked exactly the same as when her father had lived here. But of course, it didn't. It was decorated like a small suite.

She let herself in and stood in the middle of the main room for a moment.

"Father," she whispered. "I am so sorry. I would do anything to take it back."

Holding his ring in her hand, she cast around, and her gaze stopped on a closet. Walking over, she opened the closet door and looked up. There were small support beams on each side of the closet. Reaching up to the top shelf, she placed the ring behind a beam and pushed it completely out of sight.

She knew this was an odd thing to do, but in her mind, it felt as if she was finally laying her father to rest. Her guilt and remorse rose up inside her, and she began to weep softly.

"Father, I am so sorry," she said again. "Please forgive me."

"Never," came a cold voice from behind her.

Whirling, she found herself staring at the transparent form of her father, dressed exactly as the night she killed him.

"You don't deserve forgiveness," he said, "only to pay for your sins."

She had forgotten the intensity of his blue eyes.

He flew at her... through her, and she gasped with terror and a feeling of icy cold in her bones.

"No!" she cried.

Her flew through her again, and this time, she clutched at her chest as her heart felt like it was about to explode. Then, her heart stopped, and she fell. The pain was gone, but a moment later, she was looking down at her own body.

Was she dead?

The ghost of her father floated beside her with a cruel smile. "You've trapped yourself now, in here with me. I'll never let you out, and I'll never let you go. I will punish you forever."

Horror passed through her. What was happening? Had he been here all this time or had her return to the scene of her greatest sin somehow brought him back?

"Murderer," he whispered. "Fool. You killed your own father for the sake of a wastrel, and you will suffer now."

In terror, she tried to move away from him and found herself fleeing down the hallway, but he followed, remaining with her, still sneering. Is this what happened when people died? She did not know.

Flying into a guest room, she saw a woman getting ready for bed, and on instinct, she flew inside the woman.

"Help me!" she cried inside the woman's mind. "Please."

But the woman only screamed and fought to push her out. She would not listen.

Victoria's father smiled coldly.

"No one will hear you," he said. "No one will help."

And no one did. In desperation, Victoria tried to enter other people, begging them to listen. She even entered Anita, thinking Anita might hear her, might listen. But Anita only panicked and pushed her out too.

As of yet, no living person had ever seen her, and she did not think anyone had ever seen her father. So, she moved about frequently without being noticed. Often, she wished she was noticed. Perhaps someone could help her.

Then, one evening, three new guests arrived, two men and a girl, and Victoria *felt* something from one of them. Victoria watched them going to their suite, and she focused on the girl. There was a purple glow all around her, and somehow, Victoria knew that if she entered this girl... the girl would listen.

"Don't do it," a voice said.

She didn't even need to turn around.

"If you do," her father said, "I'll punish you."

Perhaps he could see the purple glow too. Perhaps he could feel there was something different about this girl.

"You can't do anything more to punish me," she answered dully.

"Then I'll punish someone else, another guest. I'll kill someone else, and it will be your fault. Just watch and I'll show you."

Victoria knew he was mad, and he would probably make good on his threat. But it didn't matter—or at least not enough. She needed to communicate with the girl. Not now. Not with him right beside her.

But she would find a way.

CHAPTER ELEVEN:

THE RING

B eth stood still as Victoria stopped sharing memories.

With her thoughts, Beth asked: *Have you ever tried to
leave the hotel?*

*Yes. More than once. But if I escape from one side, I
find myself flying back into the other side, right back
inside the hotel. He has some hold on me.*

*So, your father entered that man last night to kill him,
to warn you off of trying to reach me?*

*Yes. He's mad. The man I knew was not kind, but this
is not the man I knew.*

Beth believed this. He was a vengeful spirit now. He
would need to be banished if they were to set Victoria
free. But she needed to speak with Cooper and Lee, to
tell them all she had just seen. She knew exactly what
they had to do. They had to go to Room 22 and find the
ring.

We will help you.

Then, gently, she pushed out Victoria's spirit. This was
an easy, almost effortless act, and Victoria's ghost was
still visible again.

Turning her head, Beth saw Cooper and Lee watching
them both. She had no idea how much time had passed,
but both men appeared cautious and expectant.

"We need to h... help her," Beth said.

"You will not!" a voice echoed around the room.

Quentin Ivers materialized, and his transparent form hung in the air. He'd not been summoned, but he was visible. His face was a mask of rage, and he flew at Beth.

She held up both palms.

.   .   .   .   .

Lee had been barely holding himself back from grabbing Beth and pulling her back into the circle. For the life of him, he couldn't see why Cooper was allowing this. Cooper had *let* a spirit enter Beth's body.

But then Beth had shown no signs of distress. She had simply gone still.

She remained still for almost two minutes. Then Victoria's spirit emerged from Beth's body. Beth turned her head to look at him.

"We need to h... help her."

"You will not!"

Half-whirling, Lee saw Quentin Ivers's transparent form hanging in the air—even though he'd not been summoned. With a snarl, he flew at Beth. Lee jerked the shotgun up and tried to aim, but Quentin was rushing Beth, and he feared hitting her.

Then, to his amazement, Beth raised her hands, palms outward, and Quentin bounced off as if he'd hit the barrier of Cooper's circle. Quentin wailed his anger, and Victoria's spirit drew away in fear, hovering near the door.

Beth had not even flinched.

"Lee," she said, "run to the Jeep and get the blowtorch. Come to Room 22. Cooper, you know what has to be done." She said all of this without stammering even once. She ran for the door, pausing briefly and looking back to Quentin. "Try to stop me."

Then she was gone, and Quentin roared, chasing after her.

Victoria vanished through a wall.

Cooper sat inside the circle as if stunned. Then he jumped to his feet, grabbing up the onyx blade. "Beth's drawing him off! Run for the Jeep! I'll help her."

As he started for the door, Lee caught his arm. "Take this!"

He held out the shotgun. This would leave him defenseless should Quentin break off the chase and change directions, but he didn't care.

After a second's hesitation, Cooper took the shotgun and rushed away.

Lee ran for the Jeep.

.   .   .   .   .

Cooper hated being this much in the dark, but he had little choice other than to trust Beth. He ran as fast as he could for Room 22, carrying the shotgun in one hand and the onyx blade in the other. Somehow, Beth possessed the ability to stop a spirit from entering her. How was that possible?

And what was she doing now?

It didn't take him long to reach the river side of the hotel—and Room 22. But when he arrived, he found Beth outside the door, facing off with Quentin. Victoria was nowhere in sight.

Beth had her palms up, holding Quentin off, but he was floating directly in front of her face, and she appeared to be using more effort now. Her expression was intense.

"How long can you keep this up?" he snarled. "Get out! Get out of this place or I will make you suffer."

As Cooper ran up, Beth called, "The door is l... locked. I c... can't get in."

She was stammering again, and her voice sounded weak.

"Drop down!" he yelled.

She dropped.

Skidding to a halt, he aimed the shotgun with one hand and fired. Quentin's visage exploded. Then Cooper kicked the door to the room open. Scrambling back to her feet, Beth ran inside, toward the closet, but Quentin re-materialized in front of the door with his lips curled back and he clawed at her with a gnarled hand. She flinched at the action, probably unable not to react to the sight. But before he could try to fly into her, Cooper dashed to the side of them, aimed the gun and fired the second shell.

Quentin's visage exploded once more.

Cooper dropped the empty gun and moved the onyx blade to his right hand.

Beth ran to the closet, pulled the doors open, and reached up to one side of the top shelf, withdrawing something small. She tossed it to him, and he caught it.

"His w... w... wedding ring."

Looking down at a man's silver band with a sapphire stone, Cooper realized why she'd run here, why she'd sent Lee for the blowtorch.

But Quentin re-materialized and flew at her. She raised a hand at the last second and held him off.

Just then, Lee came running in the door, carrying the blowtorch. His eyes moved across the scene inside the room, as if trying to take everything in at once.

"Lee!" Cooper called, tossing him the ring. "Now!"

The anger on Quentin's face shifted to fear, and he turned toward Lee, but Beth cut him off, both hands in the air.

Lee dropped the ring into a small metal trash tin and fired up the blowtorch, aiming the flame at the ring.

"No!" Quentin shouted.

Cooper pushed everything from his mind except the need to banish him.

"*Ad quos eieci te de hoc planum esse videatur,*" he said, and after drawing in a deeper breath, he spoke louder, "*Et ultra non faciam nocere.*"

Quentin's transparent form hung in the air, directly in front of Beth, as if he couldn't move. The fear in his expression turned to terror as he tried to fly backward.

Lee continued melting the ring with the torch.

Cooper called out clearly, "*Ad quos eieci te de hoc planum esse videatur! Et ultra non faciam nocere!*"

The air shimmered and wavered. Quentin clawed and thrashed with his gnarled hands as he began to fade.

Still thrashing, the spirit of Quentin faded and faded... and disappeared.

He was gone.

.   .   .   .   .

Beth stood in relief, and even awe, at what Cooper and Lee had just managed between them with so few words to each other.

But she was exhausted and sank to her knees. Before tonight, she'd not known she could hold off a spirit, much less mentally communicate with one. Both acts had occurred on instinct, but near the end, she'd been struggling to keep Quentin from harming her.

Lee hurried over. "Are you all right?"

"Yes."

She wanted to tell him how grateful she felt that he'd trusted her and run for the torch and then run here. But the words wouldn't come.

Instead, she looked around the room. "Victoria?"

A blur of colors passed through the wall, and once again, Beth found herself facing the visage of the lovely, aging woman with thick auburn hair, in her black turtleneck and narrow skirt.

"Is he gone?" Victoria mouthed, but no sound came.

"Yes," Cooper answered. "He's gone. Will you let me help you cross over now?"

Casting about the room, Victoria appeared unable to answer, as if she wasn't sure whether to believe him.

"Cooper," Beth said. "Will y... you let m... me?"

He blinked. "Let you what?"

She pointed to Victoria. "Help her c... cross over."

He stared at her. "Can you?"

She believed she could. She could not have handled or understood the banishing spell he'd just used, but she'd seen flashes of memories of him helping spirits to cross over, and this act was much easier.

"Yes."

But she would do things a little differently from Cooper—just a little. Walking to Victoria's spirit, she reached and touched what should have been the side of Victoria's arm.

You deserve peace now. Let yourself give in and leave this world.

I don't deserve peace. Victoria's thoughts sounded in her mind.

You have suffered for a lifetime, Beth answered. *You have suffered more than enough. You need only to let go and let yourself move on. Peace is waiting.*

Victoria's transparent eyes moved across Beth's face in gratitude and possibly hope.

Let go, Beth said.

The air wavered, and Victoria's form began to glow softly. Then it rose and passed through the ceiling, and it was gone.

When Beth looked down again, both Cooper and Lee were staring at her.

CHAPTER TWELVE:

HOME

The next afternoon, on the drive back to Quinault, Cooper was still trying to get his head around everything that happened the night before. He felt like his world had shifted.

Lee was in the passenger seat, and Beth was sound asleep in the back seat.

She'd told them everything of Victoria's past, of Alfonse Garcia, of Quentin's murder, of Victoria's years of remorse.

Lee must have been pondering many of the same things because he said, "If Quentin died in 1979, then why did he wait so long to turn vengeful?"

"I don't know," Cooper answered. "His spirit may have lingered in the hotel, not even awake and aware until Victoria came with the ring and went into the room to beg his forgiveness. He was clearly connected to the ring, so the combination of its presence and Victoria's guilt may have woken him up."

Lee tilted his head. "That's probably as good an answer as any."

Both men fell quiet for a while. They were sailing up Interstate 5, and they'd just driven past Chehalis when Lee said, "So, are we going to talk about Beth?"

Cooper tensed. "What do you mean?"

"What do I mean? She held that ghost off with her hands, and then she helped Victoria cross over like she'd been doing it all her life."

Yes. She had. Cooper didn't know how she'd done either of those things, but maybe it was time to tell Lee about her other penchants.

After a sigh, Cooper said, "Beth has some abilities I haven't told you about. I just wasn't sure how you'd react."

"Oh, you mean like how she always seems to know what we're thinking or feeling or what's going to make one of us happy?"

Startled, Cooper almost let his foot off the gas pedal. "You know?"

"I knew something was up the fourth night she was with us. She made me exactly what I wanted to eat for dinner, again, and then suggested we watch *Saving Private Ryan*, which was exactly what I felt like watching that night. Jesus, Coop. I may not be as smart as you or Beth, but I'm not stupid."

They drove in silence for a while, and then Cooper asked, "You don't mind?"

"Why would I mind? I hope she stops trying so hard, but I haven't said anything because she's still adjusting."

Maybe Cooper didn't give him enough credit for his intelligence—or his wisdom.

"She fits into the household," Lee went on. "She fits with the two of us. I never thought I'd say this, but I kind of like having a slightly bigger family. Things were good before, but she makes them better."

Cooper nodded. "She does." He paused. "But I don't know what we're going to do the first time you and I get called into a vampire hunt. We can't take her with us."

"I know. I've been thinking about that too. We'll... we'll figure something out."

But he didn't sound certain.

What exactly would they figure out?

·   ·   ·   ·   ·

When they arrived home that night, Beth insisted on making spaghetti for dinner. Cooper assured her that tuna sandwiches were fine, but she wouldn't listen. And spaghetti did sound good.

He was just about to go check his email when a knock sounded on the front door. Lee was still unpacking gear in the kitchen, and the sound of the knocking startled them both. No one ever came here.

No one ever knocked on the door.

They both stood still for a few seconds, and then Cooper said, "I'll get it."

Walking from the kitchen through the living room, he opened the door and almost couldn't believe what he saw.

"Mother? Is everything all right?"

His mother smiled from the front porch. Her blond hair hung down her back. She wore a gauzy, ankle-length dress of vivid blue and long, dangling earrings, looking every bit the psychic she advertised herself to be.

She did not bother to feign motherly admonishment over his surprise upon seeing her. She'd not been to this house in at least ten years. He and she attempted to phone each other or arrange a visit once in a while— as they both thought they *should*. But she wasn't the type to cook Thanksgiving dinner or observe the Christmas holiday. Occasionally, she held a party for the winter solstice.

"Everything is fine," she said. "I hope you don't mind me dropping in. I just thought it was time for a visit."

Lee came walking in from the kitchen. "Katrina. How nice to see you."

He was not being simply polite. Lee had always liked Cooper's mother, and Cooper often brought him on visits because he functioned as an excellent buffer.

"You too," she said. "Handsome as ever, I see."

Cooper stepped back to let her in, but he was still caught off guard. "You just dropped in for a visit?"

She paused. "Well, I was channeling for a client last night, and when I was communing with the other side, I heard the most interesting thing. I wanted to drive up and see for myself."

Beth walked in from the kitchen, wiping her hands on a towel. Today, she wore the long yellow cotton dress with thin shoulder straps that Cooper had bought for her when she first arrived.

She stopped at the sight of Cooper's mother, her gaze taking in every detail.

But she wasn't alone in this. Katrina stared back.

A feeling of discomfort crept up Cooper's spine. "Mother, this is Beth. She'll be staying with us for a while."

"And going on hunts with you from what I understand," she answered.

She'd been talking to ghosts. He wanted her to leave. Right now. It wasn't that he disliked her. And he was certainly grateful to her. She'd taught him everything he knew about summoning and banishing ghosts. Without her, he and Lee would not be running a successful business. But Katrina Reyes never did anything by accident, and she rarely did anything that did not benefit herself.

Beth's dress had a pocket, and she pulled out her phone, quickly typing a message. Walking to Katrina, she held out the phone.

Katrina smiled. "That sounds lovely, my dear. I adore spaghetti."

What just happened?

"Did Beth ask you to dinner?" Lee asked, his Southern accent thickening a bit. "I should have done that myself. Where are my manners?"

And before Cooper could stop it, his mother was being swept into the kitchen.

.   .   .   .   .

All through dinner, Beth could not help being fascinated by this woman who had taught Cooper how to summon and banish spirits. Cooper had once told Beth that his mother wasn't a true psychic, that she was merely very skilled at listening and telling people what they needed to hear.

But soft red lights surrounded Katrina's form. Her body gave off waves of vitality and passion for life. Beth knew this had to mean something.

She could feel Cooper's discomfort, but this once, she tried not to mind. Katrina and Lee held the conversation up all through the meal, but Beth wished she could speak to Katrina alone, to ask her questions about how she had taught Cooper so much.

Katrina was kind to her and attentive and complimented the spaghetti.

Beth hoped the evening might go on, but as soon as dinner was over, Cooper said, "Beth, you've had a long few days. You go on up to bed, and I'll clean up."

For the first time, Beth wanted to argue with him, but then she saw his tense face, and she nodded. "Yes."

"I'll take her up and check the room," Lee said.

"Check the room?" Katrina asked.

"It's just something we do," Lee answered.

He headed for the stairs and Beth followed him.

. . . . .

Upstairs, Lee checked the closet and windows in Beth's room, but he noticed she wasn't watching him closely during these acts—as she normally did. She'd changed into her pajamas in the bathroom and then come to join him.

"C... Cooper didn't want me talking to his m... mother."

He glanced back. "Yeah. I think their history together has not been easy. Don't worry. I'll make sure you see her again."

It was clear that Beth had been interested in talking to Katrina, and it was no wonder. After all those years with her father and now living with him and Cooper, she would naturally be hungry for the company of another woman. But tonight, he was mulling over something else, and as Beth climbed into bed, he went over and crouched down.

"You know I don't mind you coming in to sleep on my floor, but I think it's time you tried sleeping in here all night. I'll be right next door, and if you make a sound, I'll come running." He paused. "You think you could try?"

She studied his face for a long moment, and then nodded. "Yes. I will t... try."

Without thinking, he leaned over and kissed the top of her head. "Good."

Then he switched off the light and left the room.

. . . .

Downstairs, Cooper tried to navigate his mother toward the door.

But once in the living room, she stopped. "Where did she come from?"

At least this was direct. "A vampire hunt," he answered. "Her father had been turned, and Lee took his head off. She'd never survive the foster system, so we brought her home with us." Suddenly, he felt defensive. "But we can look out for her. We've got her registered in school, and I'm arranging a speech therapist."

His mother was watching him. "You know she's gifted? Her aura is purple. Do you know how rare that is? She's a natural medium. She won't even need to use spellcraft."

"Is that why you're here? Because a few ghosts told you she's gifted?"

At least she didn't attempt to lie. "Yes. I'd like to train her."

"You mean you'd like to use her! Like you used me. Make her part of the act. With her pretty face and some flowy dress, she'd be quite the draw."

His mother raised an eyebrow. "Are you done? Because whether you know it or not, at some point, you're going to need some help with her, and when you do, she's welcome to stay with me."

He glanced away.

Reaching out, she touched his arm. "Just know my door is open."

Then she left.

. . . .

Three days later, Cooper had just finished breakfast when the business cell rang out in the living room—where it was lying on an end table.

"Permanent Solutions Unnatural," he answered. "This is Cooper Reyes."

"Yes," a male voice answered. "This is Sheriff Jason Mills from Yreka, California. Damon Tucker from Mason Creek, Oregon gave me your number. We're having an issue here... and I can't get a handle on it. Damon recommended I call you."

"What's happened?"

The sheriff went onto explain bodies found chewed up in the woods, but that the DNA traces did not match any known animals. Cooper spoke with the man for a while, and they made arrangements for Cooper and Lee to meet with him the following day. Yreka was a long drive.

Cooper hung up and walked into the kitchen. Beth and Lee were just starting to clear the dishes.

"We got a job?" Lee asked.

"Yes," Cooper answered, feeling conflicted. "Down in Yreka. But it sounds like a werewolf to me."

Beth's eyes widened. She may not fear ghosts, but werewolves were too much like vampires: strong, bloody, and violent.

Her reaction was not lost on Lee, and Cooper came to a decision.

"Beth, my mother has a big house in Aberdeen," he began. "She lives upstairs, and her shop is downstairs. She told me you were welcome to stay there if we ever needed some help. What would you think of staying with her for a few days?"

"Yes," Beth answered instantly. She nodded and repeated, "Yes." Then her brow furrowed. "But just for a few days? You'll be b... back soon to get me?"

Cooper thought he should be surprised by how easily she'd agreed to stay with his mother. But he wasn't. "Yes. We shouldn't be gone more than about four days, and I'll call you if the job goes longer. You go ahead and get packed. I'll let her know you're coming. We'll drop you on the way."

She hurried toward the stairs.

Lee's mouth was half open and then he said, "Did that just happen? She's okay with going to Katrina's?"

"Apparently, she is." But then Cooper pushed his concerns away. Beth wanted to go, and this agreement on her part solved one very large problem. "My mother offered when she came for dinner. We can take Beth with us on ghost hunts, and she can stay at my mother's when we're hunting anything else."

Lee let himself exhale. "All right then." He smiled. "So, it looks like we've got most of the angles covered, and this actually might work."

Cooper looked up the stairs where he could hear Beth packing above. Not all the arrangements were ideal, but she was part of their family now, and Lee was right.

This actually might work.

THE END

. . . . .

BOOK TWO

LOST TO THE HUNTERS

COMING SOON!

What really happened the night
Beth's father was turned?

ABOUT THE AUTHOR

BARB HENDEE lives just south of Portland, Oregon in a funky townhouse with her husband, J.C., and their two cats. She is the author of the *Dark Glass*, the *Mist-Torn Witches*, and the *Vampire Memories* series. Learn more at:

www.barbhendee.org.

She is also the co-author of the best-selling *Noble Dead Saga*. Learn more at:

www.nobledead.org.

Made in the USA
Coppell, TX
05 June 2020

27100259R10105